THE BIZARRE EVENTS AT HELLMAN ELEMENTARY

The Nexus of Strange

James
and
Sarah,

Keep it Strange!

RICHARD M. BORN

Richard M Born

PAGE PUBLISHING, INC.
New York, NY

First originally published by Page Publishing, Inc. 2017

ISBN 978-1-64027-153-1 (Paperback)
ISBN 978-1-64027-154-8 (Digital)

Printed in the United States of America

I

ETHAN WILSON WAS ASLEEP IN his bed. The alarm clock on his bed-side table read 6:25 a.m. In five minutes, it would go off. Ethan had just moved to Golfing Blue, Kentucky. He was originally from Los Angles, California. Life in Los Angeles was hard. He never really liked it. For one thing, he was always picked on by his classmates. He was a mousy-looking kid, quite small for his age, with brown wavy hair that fell past his ears. Turning nine a few months ago, he was happy to be starting third grade at a new school. The apartment complex where he now lives is called Loyal Days. It was just him and his mom; his dad had gone off to war in Iraq about two years ago. He wrote to Ethan every two to three weeks. Ethan loved getting his e-mails; they comforted him. He still wished that his dad would come home soon.

The alarm went off. Ethan rolled over to turn it off. The sheets were wrapped around his neck. He finally hit the right button on the alarm. Throwing off his covers, he set up, yawned, stretched, and looked around the room. He had only moved in yesterday, and there were some boxes still unopened although he had gotten most of his room unpacked. Posters of his favorite movies hung on the walls. His computer was set up on a desk next to his closet door. Across from his bed lay an Xbox that was hooked up to an old television set that was still turned on, but the volume was muted.

He looked out of the open window; a shiver ran down his bare back. He had been having a strange dream. As he was now awake, he was starting to lose the details of the dream. He knew there had been a girl in it, and she had asked him to come to the basement of the school. But he could not remember if he had gone or what the girl had even looked like. It didn't really matter to him. He was ready for the first day at his new school, and he was determined to make a good first impression.

Getting out the bed, he walked over to the window and checked it. He had a strange feeling that someone was watching him. That, however, was insane; he lived on the second floor. No one could be watching him as it was only him and his mom living there. She was still sleeping. Shaking off his feeling, he went to his computer. He clicked "get new mail," hoping that his dad had e-mailed him.

He had not heard from his dad in five whole weeks. This was the longest time it had been between letters. No new mail had arrived. Ethan had really hoped to hear from his dad before starting at his new school. His dad had always been a source of great comfort. He missed their talks. He always felt better after talking to him.

Now was not the time to get depressed. He only had an hour before school was to start. He needed to get ready. He scratched his freckled nose. Walking into his closet, he was thinking about what he should wear. He was a bit nervous. Having only lived in town for a day, he did not know what the other kids wore to school. Los Angeles had different trends than a small town like Golfing Blue. Ethan wanted to fit in so badly. He was so worried that it took him awhile to realize it didn't matter what kind of boxers he picked as no one would be seeing them. He finally decided to wear his blue jean shorts with a pink shirt that read, "Real Men Wear Pink."

He turned out the light and turned to close the door when he heard it. A voice had spoken to him from the back of the closet.

"Ethan." It was a soft voice.

Turning the light back on, he said, "Hello? Who's there?"

There was no answer. He must have imagined it. Turning off the light, he went to his bed, where he laid out his clothes.

One of the best parts of being in the new apartment was the fact that he had his own bathroom. Before moving, he had to share a bathroom with his parents. But now that he had his own, he could leave it as messy as he wanted. He could take a steamy hot shower anytime of the day. A hot shower always relaxed him, so he turned on the hot water. Steam was rising from the tub. He heard it again.

"Ethan."

He turned around to face the door; he could see into the closet. There couldn't be anyone in there, could there? Walking out of the bathroom, he went and shut the closet door.

Why did he have to pick today to start hearing voices?

"It's just because you're nervous," he said to himself. "There is no one in my closet."

Walking back into the bathroom, he noticed that the steam had fogged up the mirror. He tossed his dirty clothes into the laundry hamper and stepped into the shower.

He let the warm water wash over him and began to relax. The voice was probably his imagination. Now that he thought about it, the voice had sounded like his father's. This was because he had been wishing so much to hear from his dad. He picked up the shampoo bottle, put a bit into his hands, and started washing his hair.

It happened again.

"Ethan, I'm going to get you."

This time, the voice sounded nothing like his father's. It was a cruel growl. Ethan jumped; some of the shampoo got into his eyes. He was frightened. Finally, he was able to find a towel and wiped the shampoo off his face. He looked around the bathroom; there was no one there. Quickly, he turned off the water and wrapped the towel around his waist.

Slowly, he stepped out of the shower. Holding his breath, he went into his room and saw that the closet door was wide open.

"Didn't I shut the closet door?" he asked himself. "It's all in your head. You didn't hear anything, and you just forgot to shut the closet."

Taking a deep breath, he turned to the mirror. He let out a bloodcurdling scream.

On the fogged up mirror were the words, "STAY AWAY FROM HELLMAN ELEMENTARY."

His mom rushed into the room. "Ethan, what's wrong?"

Ethan ran to his mom, and she put her arms around him. He was crying as he said, "Someone was in my room."

"Who could be in here? I made sure the doors were locked last night. I think you are just nervous about starting at a new school. Hellman Elementary is the best school in town," said his mom.

"It's the only one in town. Come look at the mirror."

Ethan grabbed his mom's hand and led her into the bathroom. The mirror was still fogged up, but there were no words written on it.

"Someone had written on it, telling me to stay away from Hellman."

"Honey, are you feeling all right?" She put her hand to his forehead. "I would say that you might need to stay home today, but then you would be just as nervous tomorrow as you are now. I think you just need to calm down. Tell you what, you finish getting ready, and I will fix your favorite breakfast."

Ethan smiled at his mom. "Okay, Mom, I will be down in the kitchen in a few minutes."

He hugged her before she left. He took a few breaths and started getting dressed. Before he took off the towel, he shut the closet door.

"It had been the shampoo in my eyes, that's why I thought I saw words on the mirror." He finished getting dressed and went to the kitchen for breakfast.

His mom had made him his favorite, blueberry pancakes. She was still in her nightgown. She had long blond hair and blue eyes. They twinkled as she brought her son some pineapple juice.

"Have you gotten any letters from your father yet?" she asked.

He put down his glass of juice. "Nope, not yet. I hope he's all right." Ethan took a bite of pancake.

His mom gave him a smile. "I'm sure he's okay, maybe he is on a secret mission and just can't e-mail you yet."

She turned and poured a cup of coffee. Ethan could tell she was just as worried as he was. He quickly finished his pancakes. He didn't want to go back up to his room, but he had to brush his teeth and get his book bag.

He went into his room very slowly, still expecting someone to be in there, waiting for him. Going into the bathroom, he could see that the mirror had defogged. Relieved, he started brushing his teeth. He spit and rinsed, then turned to get his bag, which he knew was in his closet. Hesitantly, he opened the door, grabbed his bag, and ran out of the room.

Snatching his lunch bag up, he told his mom good-bye.

"Are you sure you don't want me to drive you?" she asked.

"No, thanks. I will just walk, it's not that far. I will see you this afternoon."

Ethan walked out of the apartment. He made it to the sidewalk, when—*crash*—Ethan walked full force into a boy. Both boys hit the ground. Ethan picked himself up and held out a hand to help up the other boy as he said, "I'm sorry about that. I was in a rush to get to school. My name is Ethan Wilson."

The other boy was about the same size as Ethan but a bit rounder with skin that appeared to be tan. He had dirty blond hair and big, puppylike brown eyes.

"Hi, I'm Grayson Holly. You go to Hellman?" asked the boy.

"Yes, I will be starting third grade. How about you?" asked Ethan.

Grayson looked at him, "Well, Hellman is the only elementary school around here. I am in third grade also."

Grayson and Ethan started walking to school.

The walk was a bit farther than Ethan had thought. As they talked, Ethan realized that Grayson was a pretty cool guy.

"Normally, there are a few others that walk to school. There is a bus, but the driver is a bit strange. Not to mention that he can't drive that well. How long have you lived at the Loyal Days?" asked Grayson.

"We only moved in the other day. What makes the bus driver so weird?" asked Ethan.

Grayson gave Ethan a long look. "Well, has anyone told you anything about Hellman?"

Ethan shook his head. "Why?"

Grayson looked down at his shoes. "Please don't laugh at me. A lot of strange things happen at Hellman. For example, one of the fifth grade teachers...um...um, people think he is..." Grayson broke off, blushing a little.

Ethan was curious, "Think he's a what?"

Grayson finished his sentence fast, as if it would not be as bad if he said it slowly, "A Bigfoot."

Ethan stopped walking. Was Grayson nuts? Maybe he was just joking. Maybe this was a tradition, scaring the new kid. But even as he thought this, he looked at Grayson's face and knew that this was no joke. This kid must have hit his head one too many times.

"You think I'm nuts. But I'm not. Strange things are always happening at Hellman. You don't have to believe me, you will see for yourself. Just don't let anything take you by surprise," said Grayson.

They continued to walk. Ethan could see the roof of the school down the street. They were walking past a cemetery. It may have just been his imagination, but it seemed to get darker as they walked by. Ethan was thinking about the voice he had heard. Perhaps this was what it was warning him about. Surely, the school was not as strange as Grayson was making it out to be.

He looked at one of the tombstones. It read, "Sally Goind. Born: 1996. Died: 2005."

With his heart pounding, he realized that she had died only last year and at such a young age.

Grayson saw the nervousness on Ethan's face. "Something has already happened to you, hasn't it? I promise I won't tell. You get used to the weirdness after a while."

Ethan looked up, "Yeah, something did happen this morning, but I really don't want to talk about it."

Grayson understood; he did not like to talk about the bizarre occurrences at first either. He had just pretended that they were not real. "Well, if you ever find that you want to talk, I will listen, and I promise I won't laugh," said Grayson.

Ethan did not know why, but it made him feel good that Grayson was walking with him. He did not think he would have wanted to pass this graveyard by himself. He felt as if he had made his first friend, and it did not matter to him if he seemed slightly crazy.

The boys came to the front of the school. Ethan's first impression was that this place belonged in a horror movie. The trees surrounding the school blocked out most of the sun. It looked as if it were in bad need of repair. The paint was chipping, and the roof looked as if it had holes in it. The playground was surrounded by barbwire fence. The mulch had weeds growing out of it. The redtop was full of cracks, and the basketball goal was missing its net.

Ethan looked up at the big glass doors; they had mold on them in some places. Above the doors were the words, "Hellman Elementary." They were gray, and one of the *L*s had fallen off, but you could still see where it had been cemented on.

The boys started to walk toward the doors. They passed a cracked sign that told the history of the school. They walked up the stone steps.

Grayson put his hand on the old, rusty door handle and said, "Welcome to Hellman, home of the bizarre."

Following Grayson, Ethan walked into the school. He didn't know it yet, but his life was about to take an extremely strange turn.

II

GOODMAN JOHNSON LOOKED INTO HER mirror.

This is my last year, she thought. *All I have to do is make it through for one more year.*

Goodman was a fifth grader at Hellman Elementary, and she was ready to be done with that school. She had gotten used to all the weird mishaps at the school.

Goodman's room was not like that of a ten-year-old girl. It was painted a light green. There were no windows. She had a blue chest sitting outside her closet. She was running a bit late as it had taken her awhile to find the Bulls' jersey she wanted to wear. She only had ten minutes to catch the bus.

She was wearing her torn blue jeans and the Bulls' jersey over her white T-shirt. She ran her fingers threw her short blond hair. She put on her pair of Air Jordans and picked up her book bag. She went to the kitchen to get something to eat.

Opening the refrigerator, she found it empty. Her parents were lawyers, so they were not always able to go to the store. She went over to the pantry and pulled out an energy bar. Goodman was quite skinny; she didn't do ballet or any other girly activity. She was as tomboyish as could be. She loved to play sports but hated being on a girls' team. She was the first girl allowed to play football with the boys' team. She was good at it; she could tackle all of her teammates.

She walked outside to catch the bus. It would be there in just a few minutes. She hated riding the bus. The driver, Marty, was so gross. He was a fat, balding man. He always wore the same clothes: blue pants and a white T-shirt that would not go down past his navel. The shirt always had sweat stains under his arms. He did not wear socks but had sandals that showed his big black feet. His feet always had flies circling around them. His toenails were yellowed and cracked. His balding head only had three patches of hair, and they were never combed.

The bus pulled to the stop. It was one of those old yellow buses. Even though she knew it was a yellow bus, it looked brown from all the dirt. It, like Marty, had never been washed. The door swung open, and Goodman climbed aboard. Marty looked at her and smiled. She could see that he was missing about four teeth, and the rest were yellowed.

She started walking past the rows of chatting kids. Some gave her high fives as she walked by. She sat down next to her best friend, Amy Bogen. They had been best friends since kindergarten. Amy was still putting her makeup on.

"How do you do your makeup in this thing?" asked Goodman.

"It's simple. At each stop, Marty takes a bite of food, stretches his armpit, and then shuts the door. So that gives me about two minutes at each stop."

Amy was very different from Goodman. Goodman didn't really care about what she wore as long as she could play football in the clothes she wore. Amy, however, matched her clothing from her head all the way down to her toe ring.

Amy put her makeup into the brown purse that she was holding. "All done. You know, you would look great with long hair and maybe a pair of earrings. You know, I could pierce them for you."

Goodman sat her bag on the floor. "I don't want my ears pierced. Even if I did, there is no way I would ever let you put holes in my ears!"

Amy was one of the most popular kids in the school. Goodman put up with some of Amy's snobbish friends. Unlike Goodman, Amy did not think that the strange things that happened at the school were anything out of the ordinary. She thought that everything could be explained.

"So are you ready for our last year at Hellman?" asked Amy

"I guess so," sighed Goodman. "I just want it to be over with."

Amy looked at her and gave a little giggle. "You are thinking about Benny, aren't you?"

No one was quite sure what had happened to Benny last year. He had been found in the locker room screaming about giant squids. Benny hit his head or something. Maybe he swallowed too much chlorine; he was on the swim team.

Goodman ran her fingers and threw her hair. "I know I shouldn't worry so much, but there are so many odd things that happen at Hellman. Like that frogman story, it is just creepy thinking that there is a guy hopping around the school watching the kids."

Amy covered her mouth as she laughed with her hand. "He's coming to get you, Goodman. He is going to cover you in slime and take you down into the sewers and feed you to his little froggy children." Amy could no longer talk because she was laughing so hard.

A fourth grader who was sitting in the seat in front of the girls turned to look at Amy. J. P. Milton was another one of Goodman's friends. His true name was James Peter, but he hated the name. If anyone called him James or Peter, he would pretend that they were talking to someone else. Amy called him James at every chance she got.

He was a skinny boy, about four and a half feet tall. His buzzed brown hair brought out how small his ears were. His green eyes were wide and gave him the appearance of a puppy dog. He didn't smile much anymore, and if he did, he covered his mouth with his hands. He had gotten bright blue braces a few weeks back. He didn't like them very much.

"Did you just say that the frogman was after Goodman?" he asked.

JP was big into the mysteries of Hellman. Most of the kids thought he was a bit weird. JP had always felt that there were more secrets in the school that had yet to be discovered. His older brother had vanished during his fifth grade year. He had never gotten over it. He spent most of his free time researching strange events. His parents never mentioned his brother, and if the subject was brought up, they quickly started to talk about the weather.

"There is no such thing as the frogman, James, you really need to get into reality," said Amy in an annoyed voice.

"I am the one who sees the truth, you're in denial about our school," replied JP.

"He's not after me," said Goodman. "Amy was just making a joke."

Goodman had always felt a bit sorry for JP. He lived a few houses down from her. She had even gone to the memorial service with him. She knew he was a somewhat odd, but everything about Hellman was somewhat odd.

The bus hit the curb. Amy was thrown against the window. JP's lunch flew out of his hands and landed on the seat in front of him. Goodman was bounced to the floor. She pulled herself up onto the seat.

"I wish we could find a bus driver that knows how to drive," Amy said angrily.

A dark shadow loomed over them. A boy named Joshua was standing over them.

"Whose is this?" he demanded, holding up a lunch bag.

Goodman could see the applesauce dripping off his chin.

Joshua was one of the biggest bullies at the school. He was in fifth grade but was supposed to be in eighth by now. He always wore the same clothes of ripped jeans and a white or black top with the sleeves torn off. He tore them off so that the other kids could see his huge black muscles. His head was shaved except for a small bit of hair that was shaped into the letter *J*.

JP looked at Joshua with wide eyes. Joshua must have been sleeping in the seat in front of him.

"I...I...it's mine," stammered JP. "The bus hit the curb, and it flew out of my hand. I didn't mean for it to hit you. I am sorry."

"Not as sorry as you're gonna be." Joshua took what was left of the applesauce and poured it onto JP's head. He then pulled out the baloney sandwich that JP had made for lunch and said, "I am gonna shove this whole thing up that little nose of yours."

JP shut his eyes and prepared for the worst.

Once again, the bus hit the curb with such force that JP was thrown right into Joshua. He tried to stop himself, but it was too late. Joshua fell onto the seat, and the baloney sandwich hit his face. The mayonnaise, mustard, and ketchup smeared all over his head. JP couldn't breathe; he knew he was in for it now.

Joshua pulled the sandwich off his face and clenched his fists. Goodman and Amy stood up. The bus hit yet another bump, and the two girls fell into the seat.

Joshua laughed. "You better get ready because I'm gonna get you. When you least expect it, that's when I will strike!" He went and sat down a few rows in front of them.

JP sank into his seat. "I am dead meat. I'm not even going to make it to the fifth grade." Sweat was pouring from his head. He felt sick to his stomach.

"Don't worry about him, he is all talk," said Goodman. "So what teacher do you think you will get this year?"

"Well, I hope I get Mr. Heme. He is so dreamy," giggled Amy.

"Yeah, and he is like thirty years old and so out of your range," JP said sarcastically. He put what was left of his lunch into his backpack. "I'm not sure whom I will get, but I do hope we get a new PE coach."

Goodman laughed. "We won't be that lucky."

The bus turned a corner, and she could see the outline of the school. It wouldn't be long now until they were sitting on the bleachers, listening to Principal Schmitt's lecture about how they were to act.

The bus was now passing the graveyard. Goodman looked at the rows of old decaying headstones. Even though it was just the start of September, she felt a cold chill run down her spine. She blinked; she had just seen something that made her heart stop. It was a tombstone with her name on it.

It couldn't have been real; her eyes were just playing tricks on her. She looked forward and saw the school. It looked darker and colder than it had the previous year. The weeds in front of the big sign had grown quite a bit during the summer, and vines were climbing all way up the wall.

The bus came to a halt. The three had been ready for it this time. Each had gripped onto their seats so they would not fall off. Marty opened the door for them. The three put their bags on their backs and headed for the front of the bus.

The three friends got off last. JP had barely stepped out when the door shut behind him, and the bus pulled off, jumping the curb on its way out.

They looked up at the school.

"Well, here we go. Our last year at Hellman Elementary starts now," Amy said with a smile.

Goodman had a strange feeling. She looked at JP. His brother had vanished in his fifth grade year. Was she to share his fate? Had she really seen her name on that tombstone, or had she just let the weirdness get to her? Either way, she knew that this year would be her strangest year yet.

III

GRAYSON AND ETHAN SAT ON the old wooden bleachers in the huge gymnasium at Hellman. The gym was old and had a gloomy look to it. The bleachers creaked and groaned as students climbed up to see their friends. It sounded like the bleachers would cave in at any second.

There was a huge blue panther painted on the wall. The school colors were blue and red. Their sports teams were called the Blue Panthers. Grayson played on the school's soccer team. The gym had six basketball goals and four scoreboards.

Grayson had been through the routine for the first day of school, so he knew what was coming.

Ethan, being new to the school, asked, "When do we find out what teacher we get?"

"After Principal Schmitt talks to us," replied Grayson. The first time Grayson had seen the principal, he thought she was a tad scary. "You definitely don't want to get on her bad side!"

Two boys climbed the bleachers toward Grayson.

"What's up, my homie?" the first boy asked.

Seth Chard and Justin Genty had been friends with Grayson since kindergarten. Seth was tall and lanky; his skinny arms were long and hung down at his sides. He had short blond hair that he kept untidy. He was the class clown. Justin also had blond hair but, unlike Seth, kept his hair combed to one side. He was also quite a bit shorter than Seth.

They sat down on the bleachers below Grayson.

"So who's the new kid?" Justin asked.

"Oh, this is Ethan, he just moved here from LA," Grayson explained.

"Well, it's nice to meet ya, homie," said Seth.

Seeing the look on Ethan's face, Grayson smiled, "Yeah, he is a bit strange, but he is a really good friend."

The gym doors opened once again. The buses must have arrived. It was only a matter of time before Principal Schmitt came out of her office and gave her normal speech.

He saw a few other kids that he knew coming in and sitting with their friends. A fifth grader was stealing lunch money from some first graders. Grayson knew the fifth grader; his name was Joshua.

Turning to Ethan, he said, "See that bully over there?"

Ethan nodded and asked, "Who is he?"

"He is a guy that has been in this school for seven years. Whatever you do," said Grayson, "don't let him get to close to you."

As Grayson said this, the room grew quiet. It seemed to get colder as a woman stepped up to a microphone.

She was dressed all in black, and her gray hair was tied in a tight bun. She did not have to speak to get her audience quiet; every person in the room knew that this was not a person to cross. She looked as if she were about a hundred years old.

"Welcome to the start of a new school year," she said. "I am so delighted to see so many smiling faces."

Grayson thought her words were a bit off. When she had walked in, there was not a single smile on anyone's face. Grayson continued to listen to the principal.

"I hope that everyone had a good summer. The reason I hope that you had a good summer is because it is now time to leave summer behind. There will be no more sleeping all day and staying up all night."

Her dark eyes flashed as an evil smile spread across her face as she said, "Summer is gone, and school has begun. It is time to push your cute, little button noses back into the books. You are to be here by seven o'clock every morning. If you are late, you risk failing a grade. I personally lock the doors at one minute past seven. You are not to leave the building until three o'clock."

Grayson noticed that a few kindergartners in the first row had silent tears running down their cheeks.

The principal continued, "We here at Hellman Elementary expect greatness from each of you. You will spend your days in class learning all that we can teach you, and you will spend your nights doing the homework your teachers assign you."

Grayson could see Principal Schmitt's eyes dart around the gym at the students as she spoke, "If you do not do your homework, you will be given detention. There are a few rules we have here, if you decide to break the rules, then you will be punished."

Grayson caught the look on Ethan's face. He looked terrified. Grayson gave a little giggle. It was the same expression that Grayson had worn the first time he heard the principal's speech. Many kids had to go through the principal's punishments. Many kids did not know what they were as the ones who returned from the punishments hardly spoke again. He continued to listen to the principal's speech.

Principal Schmitt spoke, "The rules are quite simple. If you disobey them, you will deal with me."

She spoke in a cold, quiet voice. It did not sound like a harsh threat to Grayson. It sounded like she would kill you with her softness.

"Rule one," said the principal, "is that there will be no laughing in the hallways. You are to walk to your next class in a single-file line. You are not to talk to your friends. If you must go to your locker, you will do it quietly and before the bell rings. If you are tardy to class, your teachers will send you directly to me.

"The second rule. During lunch, you are to walk through the line and then sit down at your table. There will be no throwing food whatsoever. If you make a mess, you will clean it up. The mop and broom are in the closet behind the stage.

"The third rule is that the bathroom is for you to tinkle in, not for you to play around. You will go to the bathroom only when you have been given permission by your teacher, and you will have three minutes to do what you've got to do.

"The fourth rule is that when a teacher, or I, is speaking, you are to be silent."

Grayson saw her eyes flash toward Joshua sitting in the first row. He gave him a cold, daring look as he was trying to steal a kindergartner's money.

"If I catch you speaking, Joshua, then you may wind up being here an extra year."

Grayson looked over at Ethan. He could see that Ethan thought the same thing he did when he first met the principal. This woman is insane. But Grayson knew that everything at Hellman was a little off; it always had been. The principal was just about finished with her speech. It would then be time to find out which teacher he had been given.

"The fifth rule is, do not go into the school's basement unless you want to be lost in there forever," the principal said.

Grayson had known this rule for a while. When he was in first grade, he got lost and was found at the basement door by the janitor. The janitor had chased him all the way back to his classroom with a broom in his hand, trying to hit him.

The principal's speech was finally over. She really didn't end it other than to tell the students the rules. She simply walked off the stage and went back to her office. Grayson stood up.

Ethan looked at him and said, "What do we do now?"

Grayson laughed. "While you were so busy listening to our wonderful principal's speech, the teachers were going around the gym, posting which rooms we are all in. Third graders are posted over there." He pointed to the side wall closest to the door.

"What's up with no laughing in the halls?" asked Ethan.

Grayson looked at him, "I think it's just her way of trying to scare us. Principal Schmitt hardly ever comes into the halls herself. She normally stays in her office, waiting for children that need to be punished."

They walked down the bleachers to the doors.

Seth and Justin got to the lists first. They cheered as they saw they were in the same class. Grayson and Ethan also saw that they would be in Ms. Mort's class.

Grayson rolled his eyes and gave a sigh, "I wish we could have been in the other class. I heard Ms. Mort is kind of mean."

Seth looked at him, "Well, at least we'll have recess together."

Grayson look at Ethan, "Come on, man, I know where this classroom is."

Ethan said, "Okay."

They walked out of the gym.

IV

ETHAN WALKED WITH GRAYSON TO their classroom. He had been a bit unnerved by the principal's speech. His day had just started, and already he wanted it to end. There was a least one good thing: he and Grayson would be in the same class. Ethan felt that as long as he had Grayson, he could make it through the day.

As they walked down the hall, Ethan looked around. He saw that in the middle of the hallway stood a water fountain. He stopped to get a drink. As he looked up from the fountain, he saw a picture hanging above him. It was of an older man. There was a small plaque underneath the picture that read, "Principal Dantzler, 1802–1857." Ethan looked at the eyes of the old man. They were a bright green. Something about the picture bothered him. He couldn't tell about it, but as he started walking away, he felt as if the eyes were watching him. The hallway seemed to go on for miles, and Ethan could feel all the way that someone somewhere was watching him.

They reached the classroom and entered the door. Ms. Mort was sitting at her desk.

"Good morning. Now sit down!" she said.

Ethan thought that Ms. Mort had to be at least seventy years old. She had short gray hair with a small bald spot on the right side. She was very skinny and almost looked like a skeleton. The liver spots on her neck grossed out Ethan.

The classroom smelled like mothballs. Ethan could see the cubbyholes on the left side of the room. He and Grayson walked to them. They hung their backpacks on the hooks. Ethan could feel Ms. Mort's round, beady green eyes watching him. They found their desks.

There were fifteen desks in the room. They were arranged in groups of three. Each desk had a name tag at the top. They also had a large stack of books on them. Ethan thought he would need a bigger bag to carry all of the books home. His and Grayson's desks were in the same group. They sat down and started looking through the books.

They had only opened the cover of the first book when the classroom door opened. A boy was standing in the doorway. He was covered in spiderweb. He shut the door quickly. The kid was breathing hard and pulling the web off his face. Ethan looked at Ms. Mort. She had a displeased look on her bony face.

"You are late," she said to the boy.

The boy looked scared.

Grayson leaned over to Ethan and said, "That's Austin Sadyear."

Looking at the desk next to him, Ethan saw that the name tag read "Austin." Austin walked to the cubby and put his bag on the hook. He then sat down between Ethan and Grayson. Grayson pulled some webbing off the back of Austin's shirt.

"I hate spiders," said Austin.

Ethan was not sure what to make of this boy. What kind of spider could put that much web on one person? Looking around the room, he saw that instead of a dry-erase board, there was an old, dusty chalkboard. Above the board were math, English, history, and science homework signs.

Ms. Mort rose from her desk. She came to the front of the room. Picking up a piece of chalk, she wrote her name on the board with her skeleton-like fingers.

"Welcome to the third grade. I am Ms. Mort. That is the name I wish for you to call me. Now, I would like to get to know you. Each of you will come to the front of the class and tell us a bit about yourself," she said.

After saying this, she pointed to a girl at the far side of the room. The girl looked at little nervous as she rose from her desk and came to the front of the room. She stuttered somewhat and said that her name was April.

Ethan looked back at Ms. Mort. She seemed to be hanging on every word April said. She seemed to be looking into her eyes. It was almost as if she were trying to read April's mind. April stopped talking.

Ms. Mort gave her a toothy smile and said, "Very good, now sit down."

Ethan listened as more of his classmates got up in front of class and told about themselves. There were a total of fifteen in all. The boy named Austin was now in front of the class. He seemed extremely nervous as he spoke. He told the class that he was from Wyoming, and his family had moved there for his dad's job. He then started to move back toward his seat, but Ms. Mort stopped him.

Ethan again saw her look deep into Austin's eyes. She said to him, "You don't like spiders, do you?"

Austin shivered, "No," as he continued walking to his seat.

Ms. Mort laughed and said, "Then you shouldn't walk past the garbage cans."

Austin's hands were clenched on the desk. Ethan saw that he was about to cry, as they could hear Ms. Mort's laughter in the background.

Ethan was the final student to get up. He was somewhat nervous as he did not like being in front of large crowds. In Los Angeles, his classmates would always laugh at him when he came to the front of the room. He told the class about living in Los Angeles and how he and his mom had decided to move to Golfing Blue. He decided that he did not want people to know about his dad being in the Army, so he didn't mention it.

He started to walk back to his seat. Then it happened. Ms. Mort looked directly into his eyes. Ethan could feel a hand on the back of his head, as if it were scratching, searching for something. He saw Ms. Mort's smile widen.

She said to him, "How's your dad? How long has he been in the Army?"

Not knowing what to say, Ethan stuttered. The only person who knew about his dad was Grayson. He knew Grayson had not told Ms. Mort, so how did she know?

Ms. Mort once again asked him, "How is your dad?"

Deciding that he wanted to get this over with quickly, he replied, "My dad has been in the Army for five years now. As far as I know, he's doing well." Ethan then sat down, determined not to look at Ms. Mort.

Ethan didn't know why, but he didn't like her. He also didn't know how she knew about his dad. He didn't want to discuss his dad with anyone, especially since his dad had not replied to his e-mails in a while. Did Ms. Mort know something?

Was it possible that she can actually read my mind, he thought. *I was thinking about my dad while I was up there.*

He looked over at Grayson, who was telling Austin that it was all okay. He saw the tears streaming down Austin's cheeks and heard him say, "I hate spiders."

Ethan asked Grayson, "How do you think she knew about my dad?"

It wasn't Grayson that replied.

Austin said, "The same way she knew I hate spiders, she read our minds."

Ethan looked down his books. Grayson was right. This school is strange. The day then got underway. Ms. Mort taught them how to do fractions and the parts of a sentence in grammar. She then gave them five pages of homework for each subject.

After the grammar lesson, she walked to the front of the room and said, "We will be having a spelling test on Friday. I will be writing the words on the board, and you will need to copy them."

She then started writing on the board. Ethan took out his pencil and paper and copied the words off the board. He had gotten to the last word—*change*—when April, sitting a few desks in front of him, said, "*Change*, hey, that rhymes with strange."

Ethan could hear the chalk snap in Ms. Mort's hand. The chalk fell with a clatter into the chalk tray. She turned and looked April straight in the eyes. She bent down with her hands on the desk in a clench and said, "We do not say the word *strange* in this room."

April leaned backward to get out of Ms. Mort's sight and said, "I'm sorry, Ms. Mort."

Ms. Mort laughed, "Don't say it again."

"Yes, ma'am," replied April.

Ms. Mort stood at the door of the classroom. "Class, I would like for you to line up in a single-file line so I can take you to the art room," she stated.

The class did as they were told. She took the class down the hall. Once again, Ethan had the feeling of being watched. As he passed the portrait of Principal Dantzler, he saw the bright green eyes and felt them follow him down the hall.

When the class got into the art room, they were told to sit at a table. Ethan liked the room as it was very colorful. He could see the teacher's desk against a wall. The room had many paintings on the wall. Some were of people, some were of animals, and some Ethan could not make out what they were. Up against one wall were wooden cabinets that were open. Ethan saw hundreds of paintbrushes and paint supplies along with paper and what looked like clay.

Looking around, Ethan saw that the walls in the room were painted different colors. The other third grade class entered the room. Seth and Justin sat with Grayson, Ethan, and Austin.

Seth looked at Austin and said, "I heard you had a run-in with Joshua."

Austin looked down at the table and avoided Seth's eyes, "Yeah, he tried to put me in the trash can."

Ethan couldn't hold in his question any longer. He looked at Austin and asked, "Why were you covered in spiderweb?"

The four boys around the table had a shiver.

Justin looked at Ethan, "Make sure you stay away from the trash cans in the cafeteria."

Seth must have noticed the look of confusion on Ethan's face. He added, "If you're going to throw your trash away at lunch, toss it in, don't get close, or the spiders will get you."

Austin gave a shiver and replied, "It is really hard to get away from them."

Ethan felt sick. His day was going from odd to extremely bizarre. He didn't even notice when the art teacher, Ms. Gott, rose from her desk.

She is like a chameleon, thought Ethan. She blends in with the walls so well.

This seemed to be a pretty easy class. All they had to do today was to color a picture. Ms. Gott even let them talk to each other as long as they whispered.

It turned out that Seth and Justin also would be walking to and from school, so they agreed to meet Ethan and Grayson after school. Austin said he lived too far away to walk; he had to ride the bus.

Seth looked at Grayson and asked, "So how do you like Ms. Mort?"

Ethan replied, "She's a nightmare! She got mad at April just because she said the word *strange*."

Grayson and Austin had slammed their hands over Ethan's mouth, but it was too late.

Ms. Gott had broken the pencil that she used for writing. She stood up and said, "Who said that?"

Ethan swallowed hard. What was up with the word *strange*? Ms. Gott, who was quite nice, suddenly seemed angry.

"There is nothing strange about this school, and children that say that this school is strange will be sent to Ms. Schmitt."

The boys looked at Ethan, and Justin said, "You have to be careful about what you say around here. You never know what can make a teacher mad."

The art class was just about over. Seth and Justin's teacher had her class line up. Seth and Justin told Ethan and Grayson they would see them later and then left. Ms. Mort entered the art room and demanded that her class line up. Ethan, Grayson, and Austin were in the back of the line. Ms. Mort reminded them all to be quiet in the hall.

They started walking back to their classroom. So much was going through Ethan's mind. There were so many questions he wanted answered, but he felt that while he was in school, he could not ask them. As they walked by the water fountain, he looked up once again and saw the portrait of Principal Dantzler. The brown eyes were staring back at him.

V

GOODMAN WALKED INTO THE CAFETERIA. She saw Amy sitting at a table eating lunch. She walked over toward her and sat down at the table across from Amy. Goodman pulled an energy bar out of her pocket, unwrapped it, and began to eat it.

Looking at Amy's tray, she asked, "How can you eat such disgusting food?"

Amy looked at Goodman and smiled, "It's quite simple, loser, you pick up the hamburger, put it in your mouth, and chew."

Goodman heard a crack. Amy spit the burger out into her napkin.

"What's the matter with it?" Goodman asked.

Amy said, rubbing her jaw, "It's kind of hard. I think it cracked my tooth."

Amy picked up her fork and started eating her green beans. Goodman sighed and continued to eat her energy bar.

"How has your day been?" asked Amy. "I've got Mr. Leech. He's kind of strange. He wants us to dissect frogs later this year."

Crumbling up her wrapper, Goodman replied, "I've got Dr. Bates. He really does look like Bigfoot. And what's up with his smelly suit?"

Amy gave her trays to a boy passing by. She said to him very sweetly, "You don't mind taking my tray, do you?"

Goodman laughed as the boy started to drool.

He said, "Anything for you, Amy." The boy walked off with the tray.

"You know, Amy," said Goodman, "you've got every boy in this school wrapped around your finger, don't you?"

An evil smirk spread across Amy's face as she said, "Yes, I do."

Goodman didn't laugh at Amy as she was still thinking about what she saw while riding on the bus.

"Hey, Amy, do you think you may want to walk home instead of riding the bus?" asked Goodman.

Amy gave Goodman a suspicious look. "Why don't you want to ride the bus? It's a long walk home," replied Amy.

Bending over, pretending to tie her shoelaces so that Amy would not see the nervous look on her face, Goodman replied, "I kind of would like to stop by the cemetery on the way back."

Swallowing hard, Amy asked, "Why do you want to go into a graveyard?"

Wondering whether or not Amy would believe her story, Goodman sighed and said, "I thought I saw my name on a tombstone."

"So let me get this straight," said Amy, "you think you saw your name on a tombstone. Do you realize how many tombstones are out there in that cemetery? Hundreds! You probably just saw someone else's name on a tombstone that looked like yours."

Goodman sighed, "I know, it was probably my imagination, but I still want to check it out."

Amy's mouth dropped open as she gave Goodman a look of horror and said, "You want me to go into a muddy graveyard in my brand-new shoes! You have finally lost it, girl. But you know what, just to prove to you that all of these strange things that you believe are happening are not real, I will go with you. I'll meet you at the stairs outside of the school."

Amy started to rise, and a girl named Caitlin waved to her. Caitlin was a cheerleader and one of Amy's friends. Amy looked at Goodman and said, "I'll see you after school." Amy walked off to go talk to Caitlin.

Goodman could see the fourth grade class entering the cafeteria. She has twenty more minutes before lunch is over. She was hoping JP was in the fourth grade class that was coming in so she'd have someone to talk to. She waited a few minutes and then saw JP coming through the lunch line. He took his tray of food and threw it into the trash can.

He then saw Goodman waving at him and went over and sat with her. "Wow, so we have lunch together," said JP.

"Yeah," said Goodman. "Amy left to go be with her cheerleader friend, so I was getting bored. So what classes have you had so far today?"

JP sighed, "Mainly, all we've done is science and math, I hate math. At least after lunch, we get a ten-minute recess."

Goodman smiled at JP, "That's awesome, so does my class. Maybe I can take you out at football again."

JP grabbed his arm. "Goodman, the last time we played football, you accidentally broke my arm!"

Goodman giggled, "Sorry about that. I'll go easy on you today."

"Actually, it might be nice if you'd give me a concussion or something," said JP.

Goodman, looking puzzled, asked, "Why would you want me to give you a concussion?"

"First, Joshua is still after me," said JP. "When I pass him in the hall, he is always punching the air and then points at me. But worst of all, after recess, I have … I have…" JP looked so nervous he couldn't even speak.

"Spit it out, JP," said Goodman.

JP took a deep breath. "After recess, I have PE."

Goodman had a pained look on her face. "Oh, I'm sorry. I don't have PE until Friday. But I will admit that PE is one of the worst classes they have here. Coach Sara is terrible!"

JP shivered and said, "I don't want to think about it right now. Let's go outside."

Goodman and JP left the cafeteria through the double doors. There were already quite a few kids on the playground. Goodman saw that Ms. Turnip's kindergarten class was already on the playground. The playground at Hellman was a really large area. It was almost like a public park. They had a nice sandbox, swings, a play structure with slides, and a swinging bridge. In front of all that equipment were the basketball goals. Past the basketball goal was a long stretch of grass. This was where the fourth and fifth graders liked to play football. The strangest part of the playground was in that large area of grass.

Off to one side was a sewer drain. Goodman noticed that some of her friends were already playing football. She and JP walked across the torn-up blacktop.

They reached a group of boys playing football. There were six of them: Devin, Dylan, Taylor, Jay, Tyler, and Peter. When they saw Goodman coming, they stopped playing. Devin was holding the football in his hands.

Dylan, who was kind of in charge of the game, approached Goodman and JP.

"Hey, Goodman," he said, "do you want to play?"

Goodman replied, "Yes, I do, and today my team will win. Which team do you want me on, Dylan?"

Dylan smiled, "Yeah, you and JP can play on one condition. You don't hurt any of us, Goodman."

Goodman smiled and said, "Okay, what team am I on? You had better stay out of my way!"

The game resumed play. Goodman had a strange feeling that she was being watched. She was barely paying attention when Goodman threw her the ball, but she caught it. She began to run. She made it past JP, Devin, and Tyler. Taylor was the last one in her way before she made a touchdown. She jumped. Taylor, being small, could not tackle her. Goodman flew up into the air for a few seconds, and then her feet slammed back to earth. She made the touchdown but was losing her balance. She fell face-first into the mud. As she pulled her face out of the wet grass, brushing off the mud on her face, a black hand reached down for her.

Goodman took the hand, and the person helped her up. She now knew who was watching her, Janitor Jibby. Everyone tried to stay away from this guy. He was so strange. He always wore the same clothes, which was a tan jumpsuit with his name embroidered on it. His black hair was gray around the edges, and his ears were about the size of basketballs. But the strangest thing of all was his belt. It was an ordinary belt, but it had a key ring.

Being a janitor, Goodman knew that he must get into all the rooms. Besides all the keys on that key ring, there was a large black key that no one knew what door opened.

The janitor looked into Goodman's eyes and said in a quiet, whimpering voice, "You had better be careful there, missy, we wouldn't want you to get hurt playing football. It's dangerous." He let go of Goodman's hand.

Goodman looked into his old face and said, "I'm okay. I just lost my balance."

Dylan came running over, screaming, "Goodman, are you all right? I saw you go down, but at least you made the touchdown!"

Goodman turned to look at Dylan, "Of course, I'm fine. I'm tougher than all you guys put together!"

As she turned to thank Janitor Jibby for helping her up, she found that he was gone. Goodman didn't think much about this as she had gotten used to the way people acted at Hellman. Sometimes if you just turned around, people disappeared.

They continued to play the game. Goodman's team was now on the defense. Devin threw the ball to Taylor. Taylor caught it and started to run. He got past Jay and Peter. Goodman was now the only one standing in Taylor's way. She saw that he was going to run past the sewer drain. Goodman made her way over to stop him.

That's when it happened.

A voice cried out from the sewer, "Goodman, help me!"

Goodman froze in her tracks and looked into the drain. She didn't see anyone there. In the back of her mind, she faintly heard Dylan screaming at her, "Get Taylor!"

Goodman's attention snapped back into focus, and she tackled Taylor right before he made a touchdown.

Sighing, Goodman stood up and helped Taylor up.

Taylor was laughing and said, "Wow, Goodman, I thought I was going to get past you there for a second."

Laughing, Goodman said, "You get past me? No way!"

JP then walked over to Goodman, took her wrist, and asked her, "Are you okay? It's not like you to just freeze like that."

"I'm fine," replied Goodman, "just a little shaken up by something that happened earlier."

"Oh?" asked JP, looking curious. "If you want to talk about it, I'll listen."

Goodman shook her head, "No, let's just play for now."

The two teams got back into position. Goodman was standing about five feet away from the sewer when once again she heard, "Help me, please help me."

It sounded as if a child was trapped in the sewer. Goodman was no longer paying attention to the game. She looked over at the playground where Ms. Turnip was sitting. Could one of her kindergarten students have gotten trapped in the sewer? Goodman took a few steps closer to the sewer and looked down. There was no way to get in there. How could a kindergarten have managed that?

But someone was definitely in there. She could hear them. Goodman took another step closer. She could now see down into the hole.

She called out, "Hello?"

She saw nothing but blackness, but then a voice answered, "Hello, Goodman, come closer. Help me. I'm trapped. You can get me out."

Goodman bent down to the sewer drain but saw only blackness. "Who's down there?" she asked.

At that precise moment, Goodman heard her name from a familiar voice. She stood up, turned to face the game, and saw JP waving his arms at her. The football suddenly made contact with her head, and she fell to the ground, hitting her head on the cement surrounding the sewer drain. The last thing she saw was JP running toward her, and then everything went black.

As Goodman opened her eyes, she felt a pounding in her head. She was lying on a white bed. As she started to turn over, she realized she was in the school nurse's station. She saw that Dr. Bates was watching her.

"Well, well, it's good to see that you're awake, Ms. Johnson," said Dr. Bates in a loud, gruff voice.

Dr. Bates took his huge, hairy hands and placed it on Goodman's hand. It was about three times the size of Goodman's.

"There, there," he said, "tell me what happened."

Her head still hurting, Goodman told him about playing the football game and hearing the voice.

Dr. Bates looked at her through his long red hair and said, "Where did you say you heard that voice?"

Principal Schmitt came into the room, looking angry. "What's going on?" she asked in a cold voice.

Dr. Bates explained to her what had happened.

Principal Schmitt looked at Goodman and said, "Where did you hear this voice?"

Goodman could already tell the principal knew exactly where she heard the voice.

"The sewer," said Goodman.

The principal's face broke out in anger. She said, "Stay away from that sewer, Goodman, or else!"

With that, the principal walked out.

VI

Recess had ended about ten minutes ago. JP sat on the bleachers in the gym. His friend Goodman had been taken to the nurse's office. He had told her teacher what had happened. He wanted to skip PE and stay with her, but his teacher, Mrs. Ragoon, had not let him.

"You must go to PE no matter how many of your friends are in the nurse's office." That's what she had said to him.

Goodman was JP's best friend; all the kids in his class thought he was a weirdo. No one really liked to hang out with him. Goodman had always been nice to him.

A whistle blew, pulling JP out of his thoughts and back to reality. It was Coach Sara, the PE teacher. Coach Sara was a beefy woman. She looked like a man; her body was muscular. She had even been a body builder when she was younger. She had crinkly black shoulder-length hair. Her face was always wearing a frown, and her eyes were stony black.

Coach Sara hated kids, and everyone knew it. Kids also liked to call her by her last name, Manley. She is one of the scariest teachers at the school. If a kid called her Manley, Coach Sara would go nuts and pick the kid up by the ears.

She had never liked JP. She thought he was a skinny and weak. She always picked on him. Today was no different. She yelled at the class to get into four lines of five. The class immediately jumped up off the bleachers and got into three lines. JP was the third person in the middle line.

Coach Sara started walking up and down the lines. She stopped at a girl named Sue.

"It looks like you will be ready for the new volleyball season, Sue. I hope you will play as good as you did last year."

She walked on, looking at the students. When she reached some of the students, she shook her head disappointedly. At others, she gave pats on the back. She gave David such a hard pat that he almost fell over.

"You have got to cut out the sweets, Mikey," she said to a plump boy.

JP knew it was coming. When Coach Sara got to him, she would not be able to control herself. Sure enough, as she got to him, she stopped. At first she didn't say anything, just shook her head.

Then she said, "You are still as puny as a kindergartener, JP."

He just stared at her; if he said anything, then she might get angry.

She grabbed JP's arm and squeezed it tightly. "I bet you couldn't do even one push-up on this thing."

She let JP's arm drop. She shook her head and moved on. JP gave a sigh of relief. After the coach inspected the class, she returned to the front.

"Class, give me thirty jumping jacks!" she shouted.

The class started doing the jumping jacks. After that, she made them do twenty push-ups.

"Well, now we should all be nice and sweaty and ready for some laps! Start running, class, six laps!"

The class started running around the gym.

JP was in the back, but he could feel the coach watching him. His asthma was starting to get to him by the time he reached his fifth lap. Looking back, he could not see Coach Sara.

Almost done, he thought.

Coach Sara was right behind him, yelling, "Move it, little man!"

JP put on a burst of speed. After he finished the lap, he collapsed onto the floor.

The shadow of Coach Sara came over him. "Get up, little boy."

JP pushed himself off the floor. "Today, class, we will be working on building up our upper-body strength. Follow me to the rope."

Still breathing heavily, JP started to move toward the rope hanging down from the ceiling. About fifteen feet up, there was a horn, and at the top was a bell. Dylan, who had been playing football with him at recess, helped JP steady himself.

"You okay, man? I know how harsh Manley can be. She picked on me before I got good at soccer," said Dylan.

"I will be okay as soon as I catch my breath," replied JP. "Thanks for helping me, but aren't you scared of Coach Sara getting you for calling her Manley?"

Dylan gave a little snicker. "I'm not afraid of that freak Manley, what can she do to me? My mom would go after her head. By the way, how was Goodman when you left her?"

JP sighed, "She was still unconscious when I left the nurse's office, but I think she is going to be fine. So what are you doing this…"

JP didn't get a chance to finish his sentence as Coach Sara was standing over them.

"Well, well, well, since you two seem to already know how to climb my rope, why don't you two go first!" she stated. Coach Sara took JP by the neck and pulled him to the rope, exclaiming, "Start climbing! Honk the horn, and come back down."

Putting his hands on the rope, JP tried to climb up. He got up about one foot and tried to go higher, but his hands were getting sweaty, and he couldn't hold on any longer. He could here Coach Sara laughing along with the class.

Dropping back to the mat, he could hear Coach Sara say, "Didn't think you would even get that far. Your turn, Dylan, let's see if you can at least make it a couple feet, though I won't hold my breath."

Dylan looked at the coach and said, "I'm not going to honk your stupid horn, I am going to go all the way and ring that annoying bell!" He put his hands on the rope and started to climb.

Coach Sara laughed. "If you are going to get even a few feet, Dylan, you will need JP pushing your feet."

Dylan reached the horn and shouted, "Hey, Coach Manley, I made it to the stupid horn. I will toss the bell down to you when I get to it."

Coach Sara looked as if steam was pouring from her ears. She was, however, looking at Dylan like a spider looks at a fly. Dylan was just a few inches away from reaching the bell. He got it and pulled the bell down. "Here you go, Coach Manley!" He tossed the bell down to her.

Laughing, Coach Sara caught the bell. "Now, all you have to do is get down."

A nasty look spread over her large face. She grabbed the rope with both hands and began to shake it. Dylan started to lose his grip. JP saw the look of terror on Dylan's face as he fell. Dylan hit the mats with a thud.

"Good job, little baby," said the coach.

JP went to Dylan's side and asked him if he was all right.

Dylan started to turn over. "Yeah, I think my back may be a bit bruised, but I will live," he said.

JP helped Dylan up and over to the bleachers. JP said, "I can't believe she did that. I know she can be mean, but to make you fall twenty feet—that had to hurt!"

The bell rang, signaling the end of class.

"Very good, class. You all need to freshen up in the locker rooms and then go back to class. Your teacher will be waiting for you," said Coach Sara.

JP and Dylan headed toward the locker room. JP went in but didn't plan on taking a shower. He just wanted to make Coach Sara think he would. Coach Sara always liked to tell him that he was a stinky kid.

After Dylan took his shower, they both walked out of the locker room.

Coach Sara stopped them. "JP, if you will please lift up your arms." JP did as he was told. Coach Sara's big nose sniffed the air. "You did not take a shower. You are still as stinky as always," she said. "You had better go back and try again."

JP turned to go back into the locker room, and Dylan turned to go with him.

Coach Sara said, "Not you, Dylan. You go on to class."

JP entered the locker room all alone. The rest of his class were already through and had left. JP hated the school showers, and he planned on not taking one. There was no telling what kind of viruses lived on the moldy floor. JP decided he will just sit on one of the benches and wait a little while, hoping Coach Sara would just go away. He sat for about five minutes, and then he heard the door open, then shut, and then lock behind whoever just came in. Surely, it isn't Coach Sara, as she would not come into the boys' locker room, would she? JP stood up and saw the familiar blond hair. It was not Coach Sara.

JP heard Joshua's voice cry out, "Oh, JP, I've come to pay you back."

JP didn't know what to do. The only way out of the locker room was through the door he entered. He was trapped.

He could hear Joshua's voice, "There is no way out, JP, I'm going to get you."

JP looked around for a place to hide. He decided he had to try something.

JP went over to the showers and turned them all on. He also closed all the shower curtains. Getting on his hands and knees, he crawled into one of the bathroom stalls. Standing on the toilet, he could hear Joshua ripping back the curtains.

"There is no point in hiding, JP. I know where you are," said Joshua.

The door of the stall slammed open. JP, standing on the toilet, looked down into the face of Joshua. JP grabbed hold of the top of the stall, swung his legs over Joshua's head, and jumped out. He ran to the locked door and tried to flip the lock, but it wouldn't budge.

He could hear Joshua's footsteps coming after him. Suddenly, JP heard another voice, but it wasn't Joshua's.

"Over here, JP, I'll protect you. You can hide in here."

JP thought the voice is familiar, almost as if… but that's impossible. It surely couldn't be his brother!

JP didn't know what to do. Either trust the strange voice, or wait for Joshua to beat him up. He decided to trust the voice.

JP walked around the divider that divided the stalls from the showers. He was back in the shower area but did not see anyone. Noticing there was one curtain Joshua had not pulled down, he decided to hide behind it. Maybe that was where the voice came from.

Joshua began calling for him again. JP knew this was it; he was trapped with no way out. He could now see the soles of Joshua's shoes walking past the shower stalls. He pressed back against the back wall of the shower. It felt weird, almost soft. Joshua's shoes were now at JP's shower curtain, but Joshua did not move it away.

Instead, he said, "Next time you won't get away." Joshua went to the door, unlocked it with a loud click, and walked out.

JP let out a sigh of relief. He began to pull away the shower curtain, but as he put his arm forward, he felt it. It was slimy. He looked at his arm, and a slimy piece of green seaweed was on it. He brushed it off and walked out of the shower stall. Turning around, he looked in horror and disgust as he now understood why the wall was so soft. The wall was covered in the green slimy seaweed. Worst of all, the seaweed was moving!

JP ran toward the door. He tried to pull it open, but it wouldn't budge. It was still locked! How could that be? He heard Joshua unlock it and had seen Joshua leave. Now he was trapped with a pile of disgusting, slimy seaweed that was moving toward him!

Once again, he heard the voice, "Don't worry, JP, I'll protect you. I'll keep you safe and warm, and you'll never have to worry about bullies again."

JP realized the voice was coming from the seaweed. He started to panic. He was not sure which was worse, being trapped in a room with Joshua or this strange seaweed. He decided he had to do something. The seaweed was getting closer, and soon his only way out would be blocked by it. The jumping trick had worked with Joshua. Maybe he could jump over the seaweed. He had to try as it was his only option. He started to run; he jumped up. He was over it and landed with a splash on the shower floor. However, he did not notice that when he jumped, a piece of seaweed tangled around his ankle. It had him and was wrapping up around his right leg very quickly. He struggled to get away, thinking he could run and hide somewhere.

JP could now hear the seaweed talking once more, "Let me protect you, JP. I promise it won't hurt much."

JP's clothes were now soaked from the shower water that had not been turned off. The seaweed was now crawling up his other leg. Soon he would be totally engulfed in this seaweed! It was now up to his waist. He knew it was over. The seaweed would take him whole.

JP had one final hope. Grabbing hold of a stall door from one of the showers, he tried to pull himself free as the seaweed was now at his chest. It was hard to move his arms. He pulled himself up against one of the shower walls. He reached up to grab the hot-water knob to try and pull himself up. Instead, he grabbed the cold knob and turned the cold water off.

He felt the hot water hitting his face. The hot water must have also been hitting the seaweed. JP realized he could breathe easier. The seaweed could not stand the hot water. JP watched as the seaweed untangled from his body and moved slowly toward the drain in the middle of the shower room.

Panting heavily, JP ran back to the locked room door. It was still locked. He could see the seaweed in the drain, but it was now coming back out. He hoped someone could hear him as he banged on the door.

"Help, help, someone help me!" screamed JP.

The door swung open. JP was thrown back onto the floor as Coach Sara stood over him.

"What is the matter, little baby?" asked Coach Sara.

Coach Sara grabbed him by the arm and pulled him up.

"Why have you turned on all the showers?" Coach Sara asked. "You are trying to cause a flood! This means detention! Now, go turn them off!"

JP slowly walked over to the showers and turned them all off. Coach Sara watched him at the door.

As he walked by the drain, JP heard the now-familiar voice, "I could have protected you!"

VII

GOODMAN WAS LYING AWAKE ON the bed in the nurses' station. The nurse had given her some aspirin and bandaged her head. Her head was still pounding. She was allowed to skip the rest of her classes that day to stay in bed. Dr. Bates had brought down her backpack and homework assignments. Lying there, looking at her reading assignment, she heard the bell ring—dismissing school for the day.

Tossing off her covers, she packed up her backpack and left the nurses' station. She hoped Amy remembered her promise to meet her at the steps to go to the cemetery. Goodman walked out the front doors but did not see Amy. JP was sitting on the front steps. His clothes were still wet.

Goodman walked over to JP and said, "You know, man, if you want to take a shower, you might do it without your clothes on."

JP rolled his eyes at her and said, "Coach Sara gave me detention for tomorrow and all because I got attacked by a pile of seaweed."

Goodman had no clue what he was talking about. "So," she said, "why aren't you riding the bus?"

JP took his shirt off and wrung out water and said, "The principal says I'm too soggy to go on the bus. Why aren't you on the bus?"

Amy, who was now walking out the door, said, "Because Goodman and I are going to go to the cemetery to find out if she is dead."

JP laughed and said, "She looks pretty alive to me!"

Amy, snorting, replied, "Yes, but you can never tell with people today."

Goodman, tapping her foot, said, "Can we get going, Amy? JP, do you want to go?"

JP stood up, and his sneakers made a squishing sound, "Well, I guess so, I have nothing else better to do."

The three set off walking down the street. There were not that many kids walking home today. Goodman saw two third graders walking down the street. She waved as they passed them.

It appeared to be getting darker the closer they got to the cemetery. Goodman did not realize how big the cemetery was as it seemed to stretch on for miles.

Amy stopped at the gates, "Goodman, where do you think your tomb is?"

To be honest, Goodman was not sure. She was just sure she had seen it while riding on the bus.

Goodman walked through the gates, saying, "I don't really remember. I've got to find it. I think it is in front of the three crosses standing high."

Amy sighed, "Well, let me get my new shoes dirty finding your grave. The three crosses are standing over that way." She pointed toward the west.

The three began to walk in that direction. Goodman thought it was probably her imagination, but it was almost totally dark as they approached the three crosses. A streetlight was all the light they had. The sun was now blocked by dark clouds.

When they finally came to the graves by the three crosses, Goodman got down on her knees to look at the headstones. Suddenly, there was a loud noise, and the streetlight went out, plunging them into total darkness.

"What happened?" cried JP.

Amy, who was not spooked, replied, "The stupid streetlight just went out, and that's all."

JP, in a panicked voice, said, "How are we going to get back to the gates?"

Amy then said that she saw a small light in the distance. "It's probably the keeper of the cemetery, the one who takes care of everything. I'll go get him, and he can guide us out," said Amy.

Goodman, who was still on her knees, replied, "No, Amy, I think we should all stick together."

But it was too late. Amy was now walking away toward the small light.

"JP, are you still here?" asked Goodman.

"Yeah, I'm still here, Goodman, I have your hand."

"You've got what?" asks Goodman.

JP replied, "I'm holding your hand."

Goodman stood up while saying, "JP, you're not holding my hand!"

JP swallowed hard and said, "Then whose hand am I holding?"

Goodman felt around for JP and smacked him in his face. "Sorry, JP," she said. "That was me."

JP reached up and took hold of her arm. Everything was silent. JP was speechless. His breathing got faster and faster. Goodman took her other hand and followed his arm down to feel the hand he was supposedly holding.

Goodman's screams broke the silence as she felt a cold bone in JP's hand. She shook JP back to reality, yelling, "Run!"

They both took off running in the pitch-black. Goodman could hear someone behind them, breathing, following them. They ran deeper into the cemetery. They could not find the gates without light. What was chasing them?

Goodman could hear JP breathing, and then he said, "It attacked me today in the locker room, I think." Goodman could feel JP's hand shaking. He was terrified.

JP's legs turned to jelly, and he fell to the ground.

Goodman helped him up, saying, "We cannot stop. We have to keep moving!"

She forced JP to start moving. They were now in the section of the cemetery where the mausoleum was located.

There was a small torch lit at the door of the mausoleum. Goodman shoved JP inside, slamming the door behind them. Maybe whatever was chasing them did not see them go inside here. She lowered JP to the floor as he started to have a panic attack.

Goodman looked at him and said, "JP, you've got to snap out of it!"

JP's breathing slowly returned to normal. "Good thinking, Goodman," said JP, getting back on his feet. "If that thing is a ghost, it won't be able to enter here unless this is its resting place."

Goodman looked at JP, "Yeah, but how do we get out? I don't want this to be my final resting place!"

JP began to look at the nameplates inside the mausoleum.

"Goodman, we're in a mausoleum that holds the bones of the founder of Golfing Blue," said JP. "We need to get out of here now!"

Goodman, looking puzzled, asked, "What's so scary about the founder of Golfing Blue?"

"He's also the one who built Hellman Elementary," replied JP.

The door of the mausoleum suddenly slammed open. Both Goodman and JP screamed.

Amy laughed and said, "What, no kiss hello? Why did you two come all the way up here? I was bringing the caretaker to the three crosses. When we got there, you two were gone. He's waiting outside for us. Are you two okay? What happened?"

Goodman could only shake her head. The three did not talk anymore as the caretaker led them to the gates. When they got to the gates, the caretaker looked at Goodman with a cold stare, "Stay away unless you want to join the dead!" The three ran quickly down the street.

Goodman wanted to get as far away from the cemetery as possible. But she still had not found any proof of a grave with her name on it. Was it real or a fake?

VIII

SCHOOL HAD FINALLY ENDED FOR the day. Ethan walked back home with his new friend, Grayson. The boys were discussing their day. Ethan still had a lot of questions in his mind.

He looked at Grayson and asked, "What is up with Austin and the spiderweb?"

Grayson shrugged his shoulders, "He just got too close to the trash cans in the cafeteria. There's a humongous spiderweb back behind the wall of the trash cans. Sometimes the spiders like to try to get kids for lunch."

Ethan stopped walking. "And this doesn't bother you?"

Grayson stopped and said, "I guess after you've lived here long enough, you kind of get used to it."

The boys lowered their voices and waved at two girls and a boy passing by.

Grayson began to walk again while saying, "Come on, man, I want to get home before dark."

Ethan still was not really sure about this place. It was a lot different from Los Angeles. There were no cars rumbling by. He didn't even hear airplanes.

"So, Grayson," he asked, "what do you do for fun around here. Do you have a shopping mall?"

Grayson laughed, "Well, if you consider the Dollar General a shopping mall, then we have one."

Ethan could still sense someone watching him. He wasn't sure if he liked this new school, but Grayson seemed pretty cool.

Ethan said, "I heard a rumor about a frogman."

Grayson turned to Ethan and started walking backward. "There is a story about a frogman that says he lives somewhere in Hellman, but I've never seen him. Rumor has it he's still there and has been there for over forty years. There are a few kids who say they've seen him. Some say the frogman licked them. No one knows really what the frogman wants. They say he just likes to hop around."

"It sounds to me that this frogman is made up, if no one has ever seen him," stated Ethan.

The boys were now at the Loyal Arms Apartments. Ethan had one more question for Grayson but did not want to ask it since he had not known Grayson that long.

The boys arrived at Ethan's apartment. Grayson turned to go to his apartment down the street.

Ethan decided to ask the question, "Hey, Grayson."

Grayson turned back to Ethan, "Yeah?"

Ethan, shifting his feet, asked, "Today when we went to art class, did you see that picture of the old principal, Danzy, or something?"

Grayson screwed up his face and replied, "Yeah, I think I saw it once or twice."

Ethan, while scratching his head, asked, "Do you happen to remember the color of her eyes?"

"No, sorry, man, why do you ask?" said Grayson.

Ethan answered, "I could have sworn her eyes changed colors."

Grayson nodded his head, "I guess it's possible. As I told you, Hellman is the center for the weirdness. I've got to go now, I hear my mom calling me. See you later."

"Yeah, see you later," said Ethan before turning to his apartment door.

Ethan turned the doorknob to his apartment. The door was already open. He walked in and saw a note on the table from his mom. He picked it up and read, "Ethan, I have to go to the store. Fix yourself something for dinner."

Ethan walked over to the freezer and took out some fish sticks. Putting them in the microwave, he waited and walked into the living room. Looking up the stairs, he remembered the events of that morning.

Was it really a voice that he had heard? Did the strange things that happened at Hellman follow him to the apartment? Was the frogman upstairs, waiting for him? The whole thing was insane. He had probably just imagined the voice this morning, and Austin must have just walked through a lot of spiderweb. That had to be it. Then his mind wandered back to the picture. He had felt so sure that the woman's eyes had changed from green to brown. How could he explain that? Was he going crazy?

He put his hand on the stairway rail. He was going to go upstairs and check his e-mail. Maybe his dad had finally e-mailed him. He slowly lifted his foot and placed it on the first step. There was a loud buzz. Ethan jumped. It was the microwave. His fish sticks were ready. He took his foot off the stairs. He didn't really feel like going up to that dark room when his mom wasn't home.

Ethan went to the kitchen to get his fish sticks and decided he would watch TV before doing his homework. He sat down in the comfortable armchair in front of the TV, picked up the remote, and turned on the TV. He wanted to watch his favorite show, *Pimp My Ride*, but he could not get the station that it came on. His mom must not have gotten cable. He started to flip through the channels.

Channel 9 was showing the news about the war. He couldn't watch that. They might say someone had gotten shot or killed, and he would worry that it was his dad. Ethan ate his fish sticks slowly as he watched *Wheel of Fortune*, the only channel not showing news. He fell asleep, sitting there in the chair. The plate of half-eaten fish sticks fell from his lap and hit the floor. Ethan woke with a start. He had just heard something.

Ethan looked at his watch and realized he must have fallen asleep. He had been asleep for about an hour. He looked at the TV, and all he saw was snow on the screen. He stretched and changed the channel, but all he could now get is snow. He changed the channel again, got more snow, but he must still have sleep in his eyes as he could almost see a face in the snow. Then he heard it once more.

"Ethan."

Ethan turned around quickly. He knew he had heard the voice. It was not his imagination. Someone was in this apartment with him, and it was not his mom. Suddenly, there was a loud slamming noise from upstairs. Ethan grabbed the remote and turned off the TV. He ran into the kitchen. He considered leaving the apartment, but it was already dark outside, and he didn't know anyone but Grayson. He was not sure exactly where Grayson's apartment was, and he thought that going outside in the dark was probably a bad idea.

Ethan decided he should hide. Being as small as he is, he slowly opened the cabinet doors under the kitchen sink. He was small enough to get in there and hide until his mom came home. He could now hear footsteps on the staircase. Whatever had been in his closet was now coming down the stairs. Ethan pulled his legs into the cabinet and pulled the doors shut. He held his breath as tears slowly began to fall from his eyes.

Once again, he could hear the voice, "Ethan, I'm coming, Ethan."

He could hear someone enter the kitchen and bang onto the kitchen table. Ethan heard the flower vase on the table shatter to the floor.

"You can't hide forever, Ethan, I'm going to find you," said the voice.

As Ethan tried to crawl farther back into the cabinet, he realized the pipes were blocking him. The doors to the cabinet opened slowly. Ethan's mom appeared at the door.

"Ethan, honey, what are you doing in there?" she asked.

Ethan crawled out and hugged his mom while saying, "There is someone in the apartment. I heard him. He just broke the vase on the table."

Ethan's mom laughed, "That was me, honey, I was bringing in some packages."

Ethan looked at the table. Sure enough, there were some large packages on the table.

"I knocked the vase over when I put the packages down. That's what you heard. There is no one in the apartment but us," said his mom.

Ethan still did not let go of his mom.

Stroking his head, she asked, "How was your first day at school?"

Finally letting go of his mom, Ethan said, "It was bizarre."

He told his mom about making some new friends and how he made a new best friend, Grayson. He did leave out all the strange stuff Grayson had told him about Hellman. He also did not tell his mom about the strange painting in the hallway of the old principal. By the time he had finished talking to his mom and finished his homework, it was time for bed.

Ethan's mom took him upstairs to bed.

He said to his mom, "Can we check my e-mail before bed?"

Smiling, his mom nodded and walked with him to the computer. She logged on to his e-mail for him and even clicked the "Get New Message" for him. Ethan was all excited when the screen showed three new messages. However, he was let down though when he found out they were all junk e-mails.

His mom kissed him and said, "Maybe tomorrow he'll e-mail you."

Ethan sighed and took off his shirt, "Yeah, maybe."

He crawled into bed. He looked at the bathroom door and saw that it was shut. He looked at the closet door. It was shut.

As his mom walked out, she said, "There is nothing to be afraid of. There is nothing in this room besides you." His mom turned off the light and closed the door.

Ethan put his head on the pillow. It did not take him long to fall asleep. He was dreaming about flying and showing all his friends his new wings. A girl walked up to him in his dream. She didn't look real; she looked plastic, almost doll-like. She smiled at Ethan, and her eyes flashed red as she said, "Stay away."

Ethan jumped awake. He was covered in sweat. "It was just a dream," he said to himself, "just a dream."

He sat up and looked at the foot of his bed, opened his eyes, and tried to scream. The girl from his dreams was standing right there. He couldn't scream because a piece of seaweed was covering his mouth.

The girl looked down at him, "You must stay away from Hellman, I did warn you."

There was now more seaweed that was holding his hands to the bed. He kicked his legs. The covers came off only to reveal more seaweed at his feet.

Ethan looked at the girl as tears filled his eyes. He could feel the seaweed now slithering up his chest and beginning to circle his neck. The seaweed would strangle him.

The girl said, "Since you didn't listen to my warning, you must now come with me into the nexus."

Ethan began to struggle even harder against the bonds of the seaweed. He looked to his right and saw the closet door slowly opening. The seaweed pulled him off his bed. The girl entered the closet and disappeared. Ethan saw his only chance.

He pulled the plug from his bedside table lamp with his fingers and stabbed the seaweed with the plug. He could feel the electricity flow through his body, but the seaweed lost its firmness. Ethan struggled against it. Breaking out, he ran for the door. He turned around and saw that the seaweed was gone, but the closet door was still open.

He heard a strange noise, like a vacuum in the closet. His feet left the floor. He was being sucked into the closet. He grabbed hold of the closet doorknob, hoping somehow he would be saved. He saw the face of the now-scarred and hideous girl. Two long strands of seaweed wrapped around his bare ankles. Ethan just knew that this was it. He realized there was no way to escape the suction from the closet. He decided to just let go and let it take him.

When he had almost given up, the door to the bedroom cracked open. Ethan then fell hard against the bedroom floor. He turned and saw the girl and the seaweed disappear into the darkness of the closet. Ethan picked himself up off the floor and walked out of the room. His mom was standing at the other end of the hallway.

"Ethan, honey, it's two o'clock in the morning. What are you doing up?"

Panting hard, Ethan said, "Mom, can I sleep with you tonight, just tonight?"

Ethan's Mom smiled and nodded her head. Ethan took one last glimpse into his room and saw the closet door slowly closing.

IX

THE ONLY CLOCK ON GRAYSON'S bedside table went off. Grayson hit the snooze button. His older brother walked into his room, saw Grayson still sleeping, and poured a glass of water on him. Grayson jumped out of bed. The water was ice-cold! His brother was always like that, but then again, he did the same kind of pranks to his brother. Grayson's brother then left the room, leaving Grayson to get dressed. He pulled on some grubby jeans, an old T-shirt, and went down to get breakfast.

His mom asked him if he finished all his homework. He said that he had, grabbed his backpack, and shoved his math book in there and some loose papers that were his homework. He then kissed his mom good-bye as he grabbed a pop tart and walked out the door. It was a gloomy day as he began walking. Grayson was glad he met a new friend yesterday, Ethan. Like him, Ethan walked to school, so Grayson decided to go and wait at Ethan's apartment. When Grayson got to Ethan's apartment, he walked up the stairs and knocked on the door. Ms. Wilkson answered the door.

"Hello," she said, "you must be Grayson." Grayson nodded his head. "Come in and sit down at the table. Ethan will be just a few more minutes," said Ms. Wilkson.

Grayson went in and sat at the table. He finished his pop tart and threw the wrapper into the nearby trash can.

Ms. Wilkson then said, "If you like, you can go to Ethan's room. He should be dressed by now."

Grayson was anxious to see Ethan's room. He thought it must be nice having a room all of your own, as Grayson had to share his with his brother.

Grayson walked up the stairs. Ms. Wilkson said Ethan's room was the first door on the right. Grayson entered but did not see Ethan. He then noticed that the bathroom door was shut and figured that Ethan must still be getting ready. He went and sat on the bed.

He looked around and thought that it was a nice room. He noticed there was a light on in the closet.

Grayson started to pull on the closet doorknob but realized that a small desk was in the way of opening it. He was trying to push the desk aside, as Ethan came running out of the bathroom. Ethan pushed the desk back against the door.

Grayson, who was startled by the sudden appearance of Ethan, said, "Oh, sorry, I just wanted to see what was in there."

Ethan looked at Grayson, "Nothing good is in there."

Ethan made sure the desk was firmly pushed against the closet. Taking Grayson by the arm, Ethan led him out of the room.

Ethan sighed, "I'll tell you what happened on the way to school."

Grayson, looking puzzled, allowed Ethan to push him out of the room and close the door behind them.

Grayson and Ethan made their way to the kitchen. Ethan's mom was drinking a cup of coffee and reading the newspaper.

Ethan gave his mom and hug, and she said, "Now remember, honey, I'm going to work late tonight at the office. I may not even be home until tomorrow morning. But you are welcome to have a friend spend the night." She was looking at Grayson as she said this.

Ethan looked nervously at Grayson, grabbed his backpack, and quickly pulled Grayson out of the apartment.

As they were walking down the stairs, Grayson said, "Hey, that's cool. I can spend the night if you want me to. My mom won't care."

Ethan just kept on walking.

Grayson said, "Well, if you don't want me to spend the night, I don't have to."

Ethan turned and looked at Grayson, "You may not want to spend the night in my apartment. It's haunted."

Grayson laughed. "It can't be any worse than the school, can it?"

Ethan shrugged his shoulders in response to Grayson then said, "Listen to what happened to me last night. Then if you still want to spend the night, you can."

Ethan told Grayson the story of the girl and how the seaweed tried to pull him into the closet. Grayson was not really shocked by this as weird things always happen if you go to Hellman Elementary.

"I still want to spend the night if you'll let me. Besides, you don't want to stay the night all by yourself, do you?" asked Grayson.

Ethan, looking at Grayson, proclaimed, "You've got that right!"

Grayson said, "After school, I'll run by my house and get some clothes. I'm sure my mom will be okay with it." Grayson could see the relieved look on Grayson's face.

The boys had now come to the cemetery. Grayson looked at the headstones. His eyes fell on a headstone with the name Judy May. The boys continued walking to school. Pulling open the front doors of the school, they heard the tardy bell ring. They hurried down the hall to the classroom. Grayson got right to the classroom door when he noticed that Ethan was not with him.

Grayson turned to look for Ethan and noticed that he was looking at an old portrait on the wall. Grayson walked over beside Ethan and asked, "Is this the picture you saw yesterday whose eyes changed?"

Ethan, not taking is eyes of the picture, replied, "Yes, and today they are green. Yesterday when I walked back to the classroom from art class, they were brown."

Grayson looked into the eyes of the portrait and thought that it did look a little creepy and the eyes did not seem exactly right.

"Maybe it's just a trick of the light," stammered Grayson. "It sure is an ugly lady in the portrait."

Grayson reached out his hand to touch the portrait. As he fingers felt the canvas, the eyes blinked. Both Grayson and Ethan jumped backward. The eyes were now brown.

Grayson was staring at the picture with his mouth open as Ethan asked, "How did that happen?"

Grayson shrugged his shoulders, "Maybe it is just something to do with this school." But even as he said this, he thought he heard something moving behind the wall.

Grayson took a few steps closer to hear the movement. He put one ear right against the wall.

Ethan started to say, "Grayson, watch out!"

Grayson turned to Ethan, looking puzzled, but all Ethan could do is point.

Grayson then felt something tightening around his leg. He fell to the floor as Ethan ran over and grabbed him by the arm. A long, pink, slimy tongue was now wrapping itself around Grayson's ankle and pulling him into the wall vent. Ethan pulled as hard as he could on Grayson's arm, but the tongue was giving just as hard of a fight.

Grayson started yelling for help, but no one came out of any classroom to help him. He was now being pulled closer and closer to the vent.

Grayson could see a blond girl walking down an adjacent hallway. He yelled, "Help!"

The girl turned and quickly ran over and grabbed Grayson's other arm.

"What is that thing?" asked Goodman.

Grayson said, "I think it's the frogman. Please don't let it pull me into the vent!"

The tongue was still pulling on Grayson's ankle. Goodman suddenly had an idea. She let go of Grayson as Ethan cried, "Don't leave him. He'll be eaten!"

Goodman pulled a sharp pencil from her back pocket. She ran in front of Grayson's ankle and stabbed the tongue with her pencil. The tongue loosened its grip and zoomed back into the wall vent.

Grayson, panting, said, "That was some quick thinking! What's your name?"

"Goodman" she replied. "I'm a fifth grader."

"Well, thanks a lot, Goodman," said Grayson as he got to his feet.

As he did so, something green caught his eye. Standing in the hallway was a man, but Grayson thought that it was not all man.

The man's skin was a putrid shade of green. His eyes were bulged out and looked as if they were set right next to his ears. He had on what looked like a white lab coat. Grayson saw that his hands and feet, which had no socks or shoes, were webbed and slimy.

This has to be the frogman, thought Grayson.

The man opened his mouth, and the pink tongue shot toward them. It hit Ethan in the face then zoomed back into the mouth of its owner. The frogman smiled as he took a few steps closer to them. This time, the tongue wrapped itself around Goodman's wrist, causing the pencil to fly out of her hand. Goodman fell to her knees as the tongue let go and zoomed back once again into the owner's mouth. Grayson knew what was coming. The frogman wanted him.

The tongue once again shot out. Grayson jumped aside and dodged it. The man took a few steps closer. Ethan was helping Goodman up when the tongue shot out again. Ethan tried to dodge it but was unsuccessful. The tongue wrapped around Grayson's wrist. He could now feel the tongue cutting off the blood circulation to his hand. The frogman then quickly jumped up into the air ducts, pulling Grayson along with him.

Ethan and Goodman grabbed hold of Grayson's legs. Grayson looked at their feet and realized they were being dragged along as well. The pain in his arm was now immense as the tongue was tightening. He felt like his hand would fall off at any minute. Ethan and Goodman held on, even though Grayson was now inside the air duct.

With a loud rip, Grayson knew that his pants leg had torn and that Goodman and Ethan had fallen.

The last sound he heard before being pulled inside the air duct was Ethan screaming, "Quick, grab his foot!"

Grayson was now banging along the air ducts. At each turn, he noticed that the ducts had a sharp edge that scraped his arms and legs. There was no escape now from the frogman. Even if the tongue had let go, Grayson would still be trapped in the air duct. He did not know which part of the school he was in up there in the air duct. As he was passing one of the ceiling vents, he heard a familiar voice.

It was saying, "Coach Sara, please get in here."

He grabbed hold of the edge of the vent with his free hand. The tongue still tried to pull him along, but he took it and pushed it up against one of the sharp corners of the vent.

Grayson heard the yelp of pain as the tongue slithered away. Breathing heavily, he put his ear close to the vent to hear who was talking. He realized that he was right over the principal's office. He thought to himself that perhaps he was better off with the frogman. Grayson looked forward and thought that maybe he was not so far along and could make his way back to Ethan and Goodman.

As he tried to quietly crawl over the vent, Grayson heard the principal and Coach Sara talking.

The principal sounded angry as she said, "That girl Goodman could cause problems. If she finds out what is in that sewer, we could be in a lot of trouble!"

Grayson saw Coach Sara nod her head, "Yesterday when she left school, she and that JP kid along with another girl went to the cemetery. They were looking at the graves."

The principal looked shocked.

"Did they find out anything?" asked the principal.

Coach Sara, shaking her head, answered, "No, it was so dark, and I shattered the streetlight. I saw them leave the cemetery a few minutes later."

The principal slammed a book down on her desk, "If she continues to snoop around the sewers, we'll have to get rid of her!"

A cold hand suddenly wrapped itself around Grayson's wrist. It took all of his strength not to scream. It was Ethan.

He said, "Goodman's at the other end of this string. We can follow it back to her."

Grayson gave a sigh of relief as the two began making their way back through the air ducts.

They got to the open vent where Grayson had been pulled and jumped into it and out into the hallway. Goodman was pacing around the spot.

"It's about time! I thought you had been lost too," she said to Ethan.

Grayson looked at Goodman, and the question spilled out of his mouth, "Were you in the cemetery last night?"

Goodman replied, "Yes, I was, but how did you know that?"

"I just heard the principal and Coach Sara talking about getting rid of you!" stated Grayson.

A shadow suddenly came over the three students. Coach Sara was looming over them.

"Why are we out of our classrooms?" she asked in a menacing voice.

Goodman looked at her, "Grayson got attacked by the frogman, and we had to save him."

Coach Sara grabbed Ethan and Grayson by the neck, bent down, and looking into Goodman's eyes, declared, "There is no such thing as the frogman! You three will follow me to the principal's office to arrange your detention for being out in the hallway."

X

JP WAS HAVING A HARD time paying attention to Mrs. Ragoon's speech on compound sentences. Sitting at his desk, he was starting to fall asleep. As he felt his eyes close, a hand grabbed his wrist.

Dylan was shaking his arm and saying, "Stay awake, man. You don't want her to put you in the lay-down box, do ya?"

Having a hard time keeping his eyes open, he turned to look at what his teacher called the lay-down box. To JP, it looked like an old wooden coffin. Mrs. Ragoon had told them that anyone who fell asleep in her class would have to be shut inside the box for an hour. One of his brother's friends had been put into it, and the kid had screamed for the full hour.

Rubbing his eyes, JP turned back to Dylan, "Thanks."

Writing down some notes, Dylan said, "Why are you so tired?"

"I couldn't sleep, I had some bad dreams," replied JP.

It was true. Every time he had closed his eyes last night, he could see the green seaweed or could feel the bony hand touching his skin. He still had not figured out what had his arm in the graveyard last night. Amy had told him it was probably just a tree branch, but he knew that it was a hand. There was no way it could have been a tree branch.

He was wondering if the seaweed and the hand were connected. There were so many strange things that happened at the school. It was possible that the two events had nothing to do with each other. What had really gotten to JP was the voice he had heard in the locker room. It had sounded like Nathan's. But that was impossible; his brother had been missing for years.

Dylan looked at JP with a curious look. "Okay, I've got to ask it, what happened in the locker room?"

JP had not told anyone about the seaweed. But when he had come out of the locker room, Dylan had been waiting for him.

JP had told him about Joshua, but he had decided not to tell anyone about the strange voice of the seaweed. His classmates already thought he was strange because of the mystery fixation he had.

"You wouldn't' believe me if I told you," said JP.

"Why don't you try me? I know you didn't tell me everything," Dylan whispered.

At that moment, Mrs. Ragoon put her hand on their shoulders, "There is to be no talking while I'm teaching."

As she walked back to the front of the room, JP whispered, "I will tell you at lunch."

Dylan smiled and nodded. JP was hoping that it would be easier to tell his story with Goodman there.

However, when lunchtime came, Goodman was not in the cafeteria. JP and Dylan sat down at a table.

Dylan looked anxious, "Okay, tell me."

JP told him the whole story. Dylan listened to the story with great excitement.

"Wow, seaweed coming out of the showers! Now, that is weird. Let's go check it out," said Dylan. He grabbed JP's arm and pulled him up.

Hesitantly, JP walked through the cafeteria. They went through the halls and came to the locker room.

Dylan put his hand on the door and started to pull it open.

JP stopped him by grabbing Dylan's arm and saying, "I'm not sure I want to go back in there."

Dylan rolled his eyes. "Come on, I have seen at least six people go in here today, and none of them seemed to be eaten by killer seaweed."

Taking a deep breath, JP let go of Dylan's wrist. The door slowly opened.

The two boys walked into the room.

"So where did you first see the seaweed?" asked Dylan.

JP pointed a shaky finger at the last shower stall. "It was on the wall," he said.

They walked over to the stall. The curtain was covering up the wall, and the water was turned on.

Looking back at the door, JP thought about running. What if the seaweed had been waiting for him to come back? What if the seaweed wanted to get him? What if this time he was not able to get away?

Dylan pulled back the curtain as JP screamed, "No!"

JP stared in horror at the bare wall. The seaweed was not there. Had he imagined the entire event? No, he remembered how the seaweed had climbed up him. It had been real, but why was it hiding now? None of it made any sense.

Dylan, frowning, said, "Darn, and I was in the mood for a seaweed salad."

The boys left the locker room. JP was glad to be out of there. The rest of the day went by slowly. He was dreading his detention. When the bell rang at two thirty, he told Dylan good-bye and went down to the detention room.

JP had been in the detention room only two times, and he hated it. The room looked like a medieval dungeon. Rumor had it that if you were really bad, you would be hung by your ankles. The room had no windows, and there were old wooden desks in rows. At the front of the room was a teacher's desk; it was covered with spiderweb as was the chalkboard behind it.

When JP walked in, he expected to be the only one in detention. There weren't that many people who got detention on the first or second days of school. As he closed the door, he saw that he was not the only one there. He was quite shocked to see Goodman at a desk at the front of the room. There were also two boys whom JP did not know.

JP sat down at the desk next to Goodman. "What are you doing in here?" he asked.

"We got attacked by the frogman," said one of the boys.

Goodman nodded. "This is Grayson and Ethan. The frogman grabbed Grayson and tried to pull him through the vents."

JP saw that the boy named Ethan was twiddling his thumbs. "You okay?" he asked.

Ethan's voice was frightened, "No, I'm not okay. This school is nuts. Frogman trying to get kids! Seaweed attacking me! I'm just great!"

JP was now looking at Ethan with great interest, "Did you say seaweed attacked you?"

"Yes, I did, and if you want to make fun of me, go ahead. I don't care anymore!" said Ethan.

JP was taken aback. He said, "I'm sorry. I didn't mean to offend you. Were you in the locker room when the seaweed attacked you? That's where it attacked me."

JP could see by the look on Ethan's face that he did not know whether to believe him or not.

"It really did attack me yesterday in the school's locker room," said JP.

Ethan looked right into JP's eyes and said, "It attacked me in my bedroom. It happened last night. It came out of my closet."

"It followed you home?" asked JP.

His love for mysteries was now overcoming him. What was this seaweed? Why was it going after him and Ethan? JP had heard of a few strange things happening to students outside the school. Could this mean that the seaweed and whatever had hold of him in the graveyard were connected? Had the seaweed followed him to the graveyard?

"Can I come to your house and see the closet where it came out?" asked JP. "We need to find out what this seaweed really is and why it came after us."

"It must have something to do with the sewers. That would explain why Principal Schmitt wants to get rid of me," said Goodman.

JP looked stunned. "How do you know that she wants to get rid of you?"

Grayson spoke, "I overheard her talking to Coach Sara."

"It's going to get me tonight!" yelled Ethan. Tears were dripping from his face. "I wish I had never moved here!"

Goodman was patting Ethan on the back. "You could go spend the night somewhere else," she said.

JP felt a burst of courage. "No," he said, "we need to find a way to stop it! I will stay with you tonight. I learned that it does not like hot water. We will fight, and we will win!"

Coach Sarah entered the room. She had a smile on her face as she walked to the desk.

"This is detention, there is no need to talk, you will leave when I am ready for you to leave," she said.

Looking into the coach's eyes, JP thought that tonight would be the night. He would figure out one of the biggest mysteries of Hellman Elementary.

XI

IT WAS FIVE O'CLOCK BEFORE Coach Sarah let them out of detention. Grayson was quite relieved to be out of there. The place had given him the creeps. Grayson was walking with Goodman, JP, and Ethan through the empty hallways of the school. They walked out onto the front steps and began walking toward Ethan's apartment.

Grayson could feel eyes watching him, but he couldn't find where they were coming from. Maybe it was just his imagination. After all, he was about to go spend the night at a house that held a seaweed monster. This night could be the last night of his life!

But as they walked on, he looked over at his new friends, JP and Goodman, and they both had a determined look on their face.

No one talked until they reached Ethan's door. Ethan pulled out his key to unlock the door, but he didn't put it into the lock. Instead, he turned to look at JP and said, "What if it's in there waiting for us? What if the second we open the door, it grabs us?"

JP looked at Ethan and said, "Well, that is a possibility."

"Maybe only one of us should stand in front of the door," said Goodman.

JP nodded, "I'll do it."

He took the key out of Ethan's hand. JP put the key into the lock as the other three stood away from the door. JP's hand was still on the key, but he didn't turn the lock. He let go of the key.

"I can't do it," JP said. "It's got to be someone else."

Goodman looked at Grayson, "I'll do it."

She started walking toward the door, but Grayson grabbed her by the elbow and said, "No, let me."

Goodman nodded in agreement. Goodman, JP, and Ethan backed even farther away from the door. Grayson's hand shook as he pushed the key in the rest of the way.

He put his hand on the doorknob and, with his other hand, nervously turned the key. The clicking of the look was almost as loud as his heartbeat as he slowly opened the door.

Grayson took a deep breath and walked inside the apartment with his eyes shut. He opened his eyes and saw the kitchen just like it was that morning when he came to walk with Ethan to school. Laughing a little from his nervousness, he turned and yelled at the others to come on inside.

Slowly, the rest of them made their way inside the apartment. Ethan shut the door behind them. JP looked at Grayson.

"Thanks," he said.

Grayson's heart, which had been beating fast, returned to its normal pace. Grayson asked, "Okay, what do we do now?"

JP looked to the side and said, "We go to the closet."

Ethan was leading the way to his bedroom. They were walking up the stairs, and nothing out of the ordinary had happened. Maybe there was no seaweed monster; maybe Ethan had just had a bad dream.

They made their way to the bedroom where Ethan quickly turned on the lights.

"It looks quite normal," said Goodman, sitting down on Ethan's bed.

Grayson looked at the closet and saw the dresser was still blocking the door from opening. Everyone in the room had gotten quiet.

Suddenly, there was a loud ding. All four of the friends jumped. Grayson saw that Ethan, breathing hard, was headed for the computer.

"I just got an instant message," said Ethan.

"Who's it from?" asked Goodman.

Grayson then saw a look of joy come over Ethan's face.

"It's from my dad, "Ethan replied.

Ethan sat down to read the message. Grayson, standing over Ethan's shoulder, could also read it.

Ethan read aloud, "Hi, son, I hope all is well there. I've been doing great. Are you having fun in Golfing Blue?

Ethan quickly typed in a reply. Grayson could read it although Ethan did not read it aloud.

"Yes, I am, I've missed you so much," Grayson read.

Grayson noticed that Goodman and JP were now inspecting Ethan's bathroom. Grayson thought that it was best to let Ethan talk with his dad in private. Grayson walked over to the window. The sun was going down now below the horizon. JP and Goodman came back out of the bathroom and sat down on the bed.

Ethan turned to them and said, "My dad's asking about you."

But then Ethan's face changed from joy to fear. Grayson looked puzzled. Ethan had been waiting weeks to hear from his dad. Why did he suddenly look like he didn't want to talk with him anymore?

Then Ethan said, "I didn't tell my dad about you. How would he know your names?"

Goodman and JP sprang from the bed. They walked over to Ethan and looked at the computer screen. Grayson was now looking at it too.

"Well, since they're all looking, why don't you tell me more about them?" the message read.

Ethan, his hands shaking, typed in the reply, "How did you know they were looking?"

No reply came from the computer.

Grayson, looking at JP and Goodman, said, "Is it possible that there's a camera in here?"

Then a *ding* came again, signaling a new message. It said, "No cameras. I can see you because I'm dead."

Ethan stood up quickly, "My dad is dead?" He stumbled and fell onto his bed.

Grayson went over and patted his arm, "Come on, man, it's probably just a prank. It's probably not even your dad on the other end of that computer line."

Another *ding* let Grayson know a new message had been posted.

Ethan did not want to open his eyes. He kept his hands over his face.

Grayson looked at JP, "What does it say?"

JP's voice was shaky as he read the message. "I warned you. I warned you to stay away from Hellman Elementary, but you didn't listen, did you? Now, I'm going to get you!"

The lights in the room began to flicker. The computer now started getting the same instant message over and over again—which read, "I'm going to get you, and there is nothing you can do to stop me!"

The friends were then thrown into total darkness as the lights went out. Grayson looked at the closet. A strange green light could be seen under the crack of the door. Something was pushing on the dresser, and it was slowly moving away from the closet door. Grayson knew that whatever was inside the closet would soon be coming out.

Grayson jumped off the bed. He ran to the closet door and pushed the dresser back into place, but something was still trying to move it. JP and Goodman realized what Grayson was trying to do and rushed to help him. They were running out of time. Whatever was pushing on the other side of that closet door was strong. They could hear the wood crack on the back of the dresser.

Goodman grabbed Ethan by the arm and pulled him out of the room. JP and Grayson were still trying to push on the dresser, but they knew it was pointless. They gave up and ran toward the bedroom door.

As they got to the door, the closet door swung open, shattering the full-length mirror attached to the door. Grayson looked into the closet for a split second and saw that the green light was seaweed. However, there was a figure inside the seaweed walking toward them.

Grayson grabbed JP by the elbow. They both dashed down the stairs. Ethan and Goodman were in the kitchen, trying to get the apartment door open.

Goodman was screaming, "It's locked, and we can't get it open!"

"Well then, we'll have to find another way out," said Grayson.

JP was close to the kitchen sink. "Maybe we can try to get out through this window over the sink," he said.

JP began to pull the window open. There was a gurgling noise in the sink. A piece of green seaweed began to shoot up and wrap itself around JP's waist.

The seaweed was pulling JP into the drain. Grayson screamed for Ethan and Goodman to run as he grabbed a pair of scissors from the table. He took the scissors and cut the seaweed. It went back down the sink. He pulled JP to his feet, and they ran out of the kitchen.

Grayson could not see which way Ethan and Goodman had run. Had they gone back upstairs? Had they gone to the living room? Had they gone into the hallway? Grayson had not been in Ethan's apartment but one time, so he did not know where everything was. He chose to run into the hallway.

The friends ran down the hallway into what looked like another bedroom. Grayson thought that this room was used mainly for storage, but he could see a little bit of moonlight shining through one of the boxes stacked against a wall. JP must have seen it also, as they both headed toward it.

The boys started pushing the boxes out of the way. There was suddenly a voice in the hallway, "I'm coming for you. You cannot escape me. I'm getting closer."

JP started to move some of the heavier boxes in front of the door.

Grayson looked at JP, "Those won't hold that thing for long."

JP nodded and said, "We have to get to that window."

Grayson finally pushed the last box out of the way of the window. The window did not look very big. Grayson wasn't sure he could fit through it, but they had to try.

Grayson tried to push it open, but the window was locked. He looked down at his feet and saw a golf club. Grayson knew what he had to do. He knew his mom would probably make him pay for the window out of his allowance, but it was their only chance. Grayson shattered the window.

The boxes against the door were beginning to shake. The boys could hear the voice now quite loudly, "I'm almost in."

Grayson yelled at JP to come on. JP ran. He jumped up onto the window ledge and got himself out as he fell onto the grass. One of the boxes JP had stacked against the door fell with a clatter.

Grayson pulled himself up onto the window ledge. He could hear the door swinging open. He didn't look back. JP grabbed Grayson's wrist. Grayson could feel the slimy seaweed around his ankles. It was pulling him back into the house. JP pulled on Grayson as hard as he could. Grayson felt as though he was about to be split.

Suddenly, the seaweed let go of Grayson's ankles. JP and Grayson dropped to the ground as if the opposing side of a tug-of-war had just let go. They were out! Grayson was breathing a bit easier now that they had made it.

But why had the seaweed stopped coming after them, and what had happened to Goodman and Ethan? Grayson knew that he and JP were safe for the moment, but he also had a suspicious feeling that Ethan and Goodman were in a world of trouble.

XII

ETHAN SAT NEXT TO GOODMAN in the dark bathroom.

"What happened to JP and Grayson?" he thought aloud. "Do you think they got out?"

Goodman shrugged her shoulders. "We need to find a way out of here ourselves."

Ethan got up and began to pace the floor. Slowly, he went to the door, opening it just enough to peer out. Turning to Goodman, he said, "I may know how to get out. In my mom's room, there's a window that we could go out of and then just drop to the ground."

Goodman looked worried, "How far of a drop is that?"

Ethan knew it was a pretty far drop but did not tell Goodman as he knew this was their only chance. Taking Goodman's hand, he pulled her through the door. In silence, they started walking toward his mom's room.

They passed the staircase. Ethan was breathing heavily, and he felt as if his heart was about to jump out of his chest. They were now almost to the room. A noise made them stop. Someone was coming up the stairs. Ethan could not see who it was but had the feeling that he knew the person.

"Ethan, I've come home, why are all the lights out?" the figure said.

Ethan recognized the voice. It was his father. Giving a sigh of relief, he started to walk back toward the stairs. Goodman was still holding his hand.

"It's a trick," she said. "Let's stick to the plan." She pulled Ethan back toward her.

"A trick?" said Ethan's father, puzzled. "Why would I be playing a trick? All I want to do is give my son a big hug." He held out his arms. His right hand fell into the moonlight from the skylight above them. The hand was covered in seaweed. The man looked at his hand, gave an eerie smile, and said, "Don't worry, it won't hurt. Oh, wait, it might." The man got down on all fours. Ethan could see teeth—five jagged rows of bright, white, sharp teeth.

The man was getting ready to jump at Ethan and Goodman.

Ethan pulled Goodman into his mom's room and slammed the door. He heard the man slam into the door. Goodman went to the window and pushed it open.

She looked down and screamed, "That's a long jump!"

The man appeared to be scratching the now-locked door.

"Well, if you have any other ideas, now would be the time to tell me," yelled Ethan.

The scratching noises suddenly stopped. The man on the other side of the door was speaking.

"Come on, son, don't you love me?" he asked.

Ethan replied, "I don't even know what you are!"

The man began banging on the door. "You will know me soon! You will be a part of me. I love children. They're so tasty."

Goodman had now stepped out onto the window ledge. "Come on, Ethan!" she screamed.

Ethan turned to the open window. He knew it would not be long before the man—or creature, whatever it is—was able to get into the room. Would they be able to make it before the door was broken down?

Ethan knew he had to chance it. He ran and climbed up on the window sill. He could hear the door beginning to splinter behind him. He could see Grayson and JP waving at them from the ground. Goodman was on the right side of the window, Ethan on the left.

JP yelled, "Ethan, Goodman doesn't like heights."

Ethan did not need JP to tell him this as he knew it from the look of terror on Goodman's face. A green, slimy hand reached out the window. It grabbed Goodman's leg. Ethan pulled down the window. The hand was severed at the elbow. The hand was still holding Goodman's ankle.

Ethan bent down and pulled the hand off. "We have got to jump," he said.

Goodman's voice shook, "I can't." She backed up to the wall, saying, "I'm scared."

Ethan looked at her and said, "You saved Grayson from the frogman. You can do this!"

Goodman had tears falling from her eyes. Ethan looked down. JP had gotten an old wooden ladder.

"All right," said Ethan. "JP has gotten us a ladder. We need to hurry."

Goodman took a deep breath as Ethan helped her onto the ladder. She had gotten down to the ground. Ethan did not think that the ladder was very stable as he put his foot on the first step.

The glass from the window shattered. Ethan fell about two steps but held on. The glass floated down; Ethan could feel tiny pieces of the glass hit his face. Two seaweed-covered hands grabbed the top of the ladder.

A man looked down into Ethan's face. It no longer really looked like a man but a creature covered with moving seaweed. Ethan was trying to get his footing. However, the step broke as he finally found it.

Ethan could hear JP's screams. "Just drop. I will catch you!"

But he was frozen by fear. The creature shook the ladder. Ethan held on.

"I'm going to get you, Ethan," snarled the creature.

Ethan noticed that the seaweed was slowly moving down the ladder toward him. He was going to have to jump. He looked back at the creature. Within the seaweed, he saw a girl. She had blond hair and green eyes. She seemed to glow.

"Go to my grave," she whispered.

Ethan did not know who she was. The seaweed quickly wrapped around her mouth, and then she was gone. The creature shook the ladder so hard and so unexpectedly that Ethan was caught off guard and let go of the ladder. He fell to the ground. Ethan felt JP's body as he collided into him. They both hit the ground. Ethan watched as the seaweed covered the ladder.

Getting up off the ground, the four ran to the street. They all knew that the creature was going to come after them. It would not stop until it had them. There was only one thing to do, and that was to kill it before it killed them.

XIII

GOODMAN HAD NEVER FELT SO scared. They had made it out of the house and on to the street. The dark clouds covered the full moon. Goodman looked at her watch; it was a little past ten o'clock.

JP was sitting on the curb. "Well, what do we do now?" he asked.

Goodman felt annoyed. She did not like to feel scared. It made her feel weak. "We can't keep running. It will follow us everywhere," Goodman said.

Ethan, who had been wiping the blood from his face, said, "I think that the girl told me to go to her grave. But I don't know who she was."

Goodman didn't want to think about it, but she felt that the way to find out who the girl was meant going to the tombstone in the graveyard where she saw her name.

JP must have had the same thoughts as he said, "We have to go back to those graves in front of the three crosses. We may be able to find answers there."

Goodman had now had enough of the graveyard to last her a long time. She nodded, "If anyone wants to turn back, now is the time to do it."

She really did not want to be the leader, but it seemed only right to give the others the chance to leave and not stay as she was planning to do whatever she could to defeat the seaweed creature.

Standing up, JP said, "I'm not letting you go into the graveyard by yourself."

Goodman was relieved that her best friend was sticking by her.

Speaking for the first time since they had gotten to the street, Grayson said, "I'm in."

Ethan was pacing back and forth. Goodman could see that he wanted to run away. She could understand; he had just moved to town and had already almost been killed.

Ethan was looking down at his feet. "I've never had friends," he said.

Goodman felt sorry for him. "Now, you do, if you decide to stay with us, we will work as a team," she said. "We will help each other out of tight jams. We need to get this thing."

Goodman could see that Ethan was ready to fight as he said, "No one impersonates my dad and gets away with it. Let's send this thing to the great beyond!"

Goodman felt somewhat better as they walked up the street to the cemetery. She knew that she would be okay as long as she had her friends with her. As they got closer to the graveyard, Goodman felt as if someone was watching them. They entered the dark cemetery and started toward the three crosses.

When they were about halfway, Goodman stopped. The others also stopped. She had heard footsteps, and who or whatever they belonged to had not realized they had stopped.

"Did you hear that?" asked Grayson.

Goodman looked at him and replied, "Yeah."

They continued walking. She could now see the large tombstone that she thought she had seen that had her name on it. She stopped walking again.

"I can't look," she said. "What if my name is on it?"

Ethan took a deep breath and said, "I will look."

Goodman knew that Ethan was doing this because of the fact she had told him they were friends. He walked around to the front side of the tombstone. Goodman could see him bend down and wipe away some spiderweb.

Crossing her fingers, Goodman wondered what name would be on the tombstone. Was it going to be hers? If so, what did that mean? She wasn't dead. If someone had put her name on the tombstone, then did that mean somebody wanted her dead?

Ethan suddenly gasped.

"What?" yelled Goodman. "Whose name is on there?" She was starting to panic.

Ethan stood up, saying, "This is the grave that I saw on my first day here. It's a young girl named Sally Grind."

Relief washed over Goodman. It was not her name, and that was great news. "Does it say how she died?" she asked.

"No, it just says that she was a beloved daughter," said Ethan.

"I can tell you how she died, the same way you four will die," said a gruff voice.

The person was drowned in the shadows, but Goodman could tell who that person was. Coach Sara grabbed JP and Grayson by the neck.

Grayson had just enough time to scream, "Run!"

Goodman and Ethan took off running. They were weaving around the graves while all the time hearing Coach Sara laughing. They hid behind an old oak tree. They saw Coach Sara taking Grayson and JP into the old chapel.

"We have got to get them out," said Ethan.

Goodman looked at him. "Have you got any thoughts on how to do that?" she asked.

"Not a clue," he replied. "Do you think that Coach Sara is the seaweed monster?" Ethan asked Goodman.

"No, I don't," said Goodman. "She may be mean, but I don't think she is made of seaweed. I do think that she knows what the seaweed thing is, though."

Ethan stood up and took a deep breath and said, "I am brave! You go and get JP and Grayson. I will keep Coach Sara occupied. You guys meet me at the gate."

"Are you sure about this?" asked Goodman. "What if you get caught?

"I'm fast, and I'm small, which gives me a big advantage against Coach Wacko!" declared Ethan.

Goodman knew that it was a risky move, but there was really no other choice. "Okay," she agreed.

They slowly crept toward the chapel. Goodman thought that she had seen Coach Sara through a window. When they got to the chapel window, they saw Coach Sara tying Grayson and JP to a chair.

"How are you going to undo the knot?" asked Ethan.

"I've got a pocket knife," Goodman replied.

"Okay, you need to be hidden so Coach Sara won't come after you," said Ethan.

Goodman swallowed hard and nodded. She ducked down and crawled into a bush. She felt itchy and hoped she had not gotten into anything poisonous.

Goodman had a clear view of Ethan through a gap in the branches of the bush. He was walking to the front doors.

His voice echoed into the night, "Hey, Manley, come on out and get me—that is, if you can catch me on those legs of yours!"

Goodman was surprised that such a little guy could have such a loud voice.

"Come on, ugly, you have a face only a mama would love! That's why you've got the name Manley!" continued Ethan.

The doors of the chapel burst open. There in the doorway stood Coach Sara. She was breathing hard. Her chest was heaving up and down.

"I'm going to rip off your limbs with my Manley muscles!" she screamed.

Goodman watched as Coach Sara ran at Ethan. Ethan was not lying when he said he could run fast. She watched as he ran away from the coach. He was jumping over tombstones. Coach Sara chased after him. Now was her chance. Goodman crawled out of the bush.

She could still hear Ethan yelling, "Manley, oh, Manley, you can't get me!"

Goodman had made it to the chapel doors. They must have locked behind Coach Sara. She had to find a way inside. She looked around for a side door. All she saw was a stained glass window. It was her only way into the chapel. She had to move fast. Coach Sara could be back any minute.

Goodman picked up a large rock and shattered the window. She pulled herself up, but she had cut her hand on a bit of glass. She had made it into the chapel! Now all she had to do was get to her friends.

Pulling a small piece of stained glass out of her hand, Goodman entered into the chapel's hallway. She had gotten turned around. Where was the room that JP and Grayson were in?

Goodman began walking to the left. Up ahead was a strange-looking glow that was coming from the cracks of a closed door. Hoping that her friends were in this room, she opened the door. It took a few seconds for her eyes to adjust.

Standing in the middle of the room was a young, beautiful girl. She was bathed in the strange, glowing light. Goodman recognized her from the ladder at Ethan's apartment.

"Who are you?" asked Goodman.

The girl smiled, "You already know. You must help me. My spirit cannot move on. He is going to come after you. He must be stopped!"

Goodman could fee a chill run up her spine as she asked, "You are Sally, aren't you?"

"Yes, your friends are two doors to the right. Please help me," said Sally before she disappeared.

Goodman stood in shock for a moment before remembering that she had to get to her friends. She raced down the hall. Slowly, she opened the door.

"Goodman!" cried JP. He and Grayson were tied to a chair.

"What happened to Ethan?" asked Grayson.

Goodman went to Grayson's chair and pulled out a small pocket knife. "He is keeping that buffoon Manley busy," she said as she started to cut the ropes.

A man-sized hands suddenly grabbed Goodman's wrist. The knife fell to the floor.

Goodman looked into the face of Coach Sara as she said, "The buffoon came back."

Goodman felt that her wrist was about to break.

Coach Sara lifted her up off the floor while saying, "I knew you would come to help your friends. Now you will suffer the same fate!"

XIV

JP COULD FEEL GRAYSON STRUGGLING against his ropes as Coach Sara was tying up Goodman. He could see no way out as the ropes were too tight. JP had seen Coach Sara get angry before, but looking at her face now was scary. She normally had her hair neat, but tonight it was sticking up all over. He even thought that her eyes were filled with evil.

JP was trying to push Ethan out of his mind. Had he gotten away? Had Coach Sara done something to him?

He took a deep breath and said, "Okay, you have a captive audience. Now why don't you tell us why you are doing this?"

Coach Sara finished tying Goodman to the chair. She then turned to JP. What JP had seen in her eyes was wrong. They didn't look evil; they had the appearance of a person who was terrified. She grabbed Grayson's shoulders to stop him from moving.

"Don't waste your energy," she said.

JP knew what he was about to do was stupid, but he wanted answers. "You're scared of something! That's it—the big, scary gym teacher is scared. So what are you afraid of, Manley?"

It happened fast. JP wasn't even sure how Coach Sara had gotten in front of him. The coach's hand was around his throat. "Shut up, you stupid brat, or I will kill you," she said. She let go of JP.

Coughing a bit, JP continued, "Kill me? If you're not going to kill us, what are you going to do? Maybe you will make us do jumping jacks or push-ups, sit-ups maybe. Oh, wait, we are tied up, so I guess that's not going to happen."

Goodman and Grayson were looking at JP.

"What are you doing?" asked Grayson.

JP ignored him and went on, yelling, "So what is stopping you from killing us? What has Coach Sara shaking in her boots? Maybe if you kill us, that stupid seaweed thing will kill you!"

The anger in the coach's eyes was pronounced. "I told you to shut up! Do not insult Salmoa!" she exclaimed.

Grayson had stopped struggling against his ropes. Goodman was looking back and forth at JP and Coach Sara.

Coach Sara's face had turned bright red. Her eyes were bulging out, and her fists were clenched.

JP was afraid that Coach Sara was going to hit him, but he went on talking, "Does that thing have a name?"

"Of course, he has a name. He is one of the greatest monsters who have ever come to the school," stated Coach Sara. "He has been feeding on the kids of Hellman for ages. He takes two children every five years. This year he wants you, JP, and the new kid!"

JP looked at her. "And you are helping him get us, aren't you?"

Coach Sara's smile turned nasty. "Yes, I am. I've been helping him for years."

It was as if the fog had lifted from JP's brain. Everything fell into place. He finally understood. "You helped kill Sally Grind, didn't you?" he asked.

Coach Sara laughed a dark, cold laugh and replied, "No, Sally died because she went up against him."

JP was going to say something, but it now looked like his plan had worked. Coach Sara was now telling them everything.

"Sally's brother was scarified to Salmoa," explained the coach. "She would not give up trying to find her brother. Once she found out that Salmoa had killed him, she wanted revenge."

Coach Sara said, "It took her a few months to find out where Salmoa lived. She learned that the creature lived in the sewers underneath the school. She supposedly found a way to kill it. But when she went to fight it, she never came back. The place where she died was the boys' locker room. The principal and I had a hard time making it look like an accident, but we pulled it off, and Salmoa was happy."

JP looked at Goodman. He thought she was about to be sick. Grayson had started struggling against the ropes once more. Coach

Sara did not seem grief-stricken about Sally's death. Although JP did not personally know Sally, he knew how it felt to find out that your brother had died.

Was it Salmoa that took my own brother? he thought. But his brother did not die in the boys' locker room.

Coach Sara continued, "Salmoa has rewarded me, and now I will get to give him three troublemakers, and he will enjoy feeding on you!"

JP had a thought, and he said what came to his mind, "But Salmoa wanted Ethan and me. You may be able to give him me, but you haven't caught Ethan yet."

A flicker of fear spread through Coach Sara's face as she said, "No, not yet. But I'll get him, and then Salmoa will have four children to feed on for the next five years!"

JP was now beginning to get scared. He had run out of things to keep Coach Sara talking. He knew that Salmoa would be coming for them soon. A thought went through his head about Ethan.

If Coach Sara had not gotten him, where was he? Had Salmoa already gotten his first victim?

There was suddenly a loud crash, and someone came flying through the upper stained glass window of the chapel. Coach Sara was knocked to the floor. Ethan was on top of her.

Goodman, Grayson, and JP all screamed, "Ethan!"

Ethan climbed off Coach Sara. Grabbing a piece of the broken stained glass, he started hacking at JP's ropes. Once JP was freed, he grabbed the pocket knife out of Coach Sara's pocket and started finishing cutting the ropes binding Grayson while Ethan was hacking at Goodman's bonds.

Ethan looked at them and said, "You know, you guys kept me waiting for so long that I had to come back and see what was keeping you."

Goodman smiled and said, "Thanks for coming back. But how did you outrun Coach Sara?"

Ethan laughed, "That was the easy part. Figuring how to get you guys out of here was the hard part."

Coach Sara had now made it back onto her feet. "Good. Now all four of you can die together!"

The front doors of the chapel clanged open, and there stood Salmoa, dripping wet seaweed. He looked like a man. He slowly approached Coach Sara. His voice was harsh and demanding—not like the kind, gentle voice JP had heard in the boys' locker room.

His eyes were bright red as he moved his hand toward Coach Sara. "You have failed me, Manley, and I will deal with you later! As for now, I have grown hungry." He started walking toward JP.

JP and the others slowly backed into the altar.

How were they going to get out of this one? JP thought.

They were trapped, and there was no way to get around the slimy creature now approaching them. It was over. But a memory came into JP's mind—a memory of seeing the scalding hot water hit the seaweed and it backing down the drain in the boys' locker room.

JP then had an idea. It was a long shot, but hey, they were in a chapel. There had to be a lit candle somewhere. He looked around, and sure enough, about ten feet away was a lit candle.

Ethan was thinking along the same lines as JP. Ethan sprinted toward the candle. JP appreciated how fast Ethan could move. Ethan now had the candle in his hands. Salmoa stopped walking toward them. Ethan grabbed three other candles that were not lit.

Ethan slowly walked back over to the others while Salmoa kept his eyes on Ethan. Ethan handed JP one of the candles and lit it with his lit candle. He did the same for Goodman and Grayson.

Salmoa's eyes were wide with fear. JP looked around. The only way out was through the doorway that Goodman had come in. But they only had one chance.

JP turned to the others and said, "On the count of three, run. If the seaweed gets too close, burn it with the candlelight."

JP started counting, "One." Salmoa was looking anxious, but he was now slowly beginning to approach them again. JP continued, "Two." Salmoa was getting closer. "Three!" screamed JP.

Ethan, Goodman, and Grayson all ran toward the door. JP followed.

Once JP got to the door, he turned around and saw Salmoa chasing after them. He knew he would be in trouble for doing what he was about to do. It was the only way to give them enough time to get out. He put the flickering candle flame next to the doorway. The wooden door frame caught fire.

JP then threw the candle at Salmoa and ran to join the others. As they were all running down the hall toward the shattered window that Goodman had come through, they could hear Salmoa screaming at Coach Sara, "You let them escape! You will now come with me, and you will pay dearly for this!"

JP and the others were now back in the graveyard.

Ethan said, "It's afraid of fire, afraid of the warmth. That's how we have to kill it."

Grayson look at him, "But how do we find out where he is?"

Goodman looked at Grayson, "Coach Sara told us. We have to go into the sewer, the sewer in the soccer field of Hellman."

X

GRAYSON WAS NOW PANTING HARD. His hands were on his knees; he felt like he was going to be sick. They had now made it out of the graveyard and were back onto the dimly lit street. Grayson was not sure what had happened to Coach Sara, but at the moment, he didn't really care.

Grayson, looking at the others, said, "He will not stop until he gets all of us."

Goodman sighed, "That's why we have to get him before he gets us!"

Grayson, looking annoyed, asked, "And how are we going to get him?"

JP, who was still breathing quite hard, said, "We know he is afraid of fire. All we have to do is hit him with enough fire to kill him."

Grayson rolled his eyes, "And where are we going to get enough fire power to kill him? We're kids! They don't sell hand grenades to ten-year-olds!"

Ethan looked at Grayson, "I don't think we're going to need hand grenades. I think something a little less obvious will do the trick. Something that Salmoa won't be suspecting."

Goodman, looking puzzled, asked, "What did you have in mind, Ethan?"

Ethan looked at his new friends and said, "Fireworks!"

Grayson looked at Ethan, "How is that going to work?"

Ethan shrugged his shoulders, "Well, the way I see it is we go down to the sewers and find out where that creature is living. We set off the fireworks, and hopefully, it will give off enough heat to kill Salmoa. But this may just be a stupid idea."

JP was laughing. "No, it's a brilliant idea! But where are we going to get a great a number of fireworks?"

Grayson replied, "My brother has been saving fireworks for years. He's been buying bottle rockets, Roman candles, just about anything you can think of. Man, is he going to be angry when he finds out that I'm the one who stole them!"

Goodman looked at Grayson, "Don't worry, we'll help you buy his fireworks back."

Grayson said excitedly, "Then in that case, we had better get going."

JP looked at the others for a second and then said, "I think we should split up. Two of us should get the fireworks, the other two need to figure out how we are going to get into the sewer without getting caught."

Ethan saw the scared look on Grayson's face and stated, "I will go with Grayson."

"Okay," said JP. "Meet in front of the school in one hour."

Grayson and Ethan watched as JP and Goodman disappeared into the darkness, heading for the school. Grayson had a feeling of being watched, but he wasn't sure by whom. This whole night was becoming worse and worse. He and Ethan were now walking toward his house. When they reached the house, Grayson and Ethan slowly opened the front door.

Grayson whispered to Ethan, "Let's keep it quiet so my parents and brother do not wake up."

Ethan slowly crept through the house with Grayson. They came to a small hallway closet.

Grayson slowly opened the closet door and pulled out two backpacks. He then pulled down a large box from the upper shelf and began to pull out fireworks from the box. He handed Ethan a backpack once it was filled. After filling the second backpack, he put it on his back. The boys then silently crept back down the hallway and out the front door.

Grayson and Ethan made their way back to the school. Once there, they could not find JP and Grayson.

Ethan looked at Grayson and said, "You don't think they got caught, do you?"

JP stepped out from behind a tree. "Us getting caught? How ridiculous!"

Goodman then came out, saying, "It's good to see that you two are okay. We were getting worried."

Grayson looked at Goodman, "Have you two found a way into the sewer yet?"

Goodman replied, "Not yet, but about fifteen minutes ago, we saw Salmoa taking what looked to be a body down into the sewer."

Ethan said, "It must have been Coach Sara. Do you think he killed her?"

JP looked at him, "Don't really know. We couldn't tell much from all the way over here."

"The grate that is covering the sewer," said Goodman, "has got a lock on it. We will need a key to get in."

Grayson thought he already knew the answer to his question, but he had to ask, "And where are we going to get the key?"

JP hit his head with his hand, "We are going to do one of the dumbest things a student at Hellman has ever done. We're going to break into the principal's office."

Grayson declared, "Oh, great! That's another crime we're going to commit."

JP replied, "Well, at least you didn't burn down the chapel."

Grayson looked at Goodman, "Well, if we need a key, how did Salmoa and Coach Sara get down there?"

JP scratched his head and said, "Well, he wrapped Coach Sara in seaweed, and then they just slid through the bars."

Goodman put her hand over her mouth and moaned, "It was sickening."

Ethan, who was pacing again, said, "Can we please get on with this?"

Grayson looked at the dark front doors of the school. The memory of being attacked by the frogman was all he could think about.

"What if going in there is another trap? I mean, what if the frogman is waiting to get us?"

Goodman started walking toward the doors. "Fine, I will go in alone." She put her hand on the door.

Ethan called, "No, wait!" Goodman turned around as Ethan joined her on the steps. "No one goes alone."

JP joined them, and so did a reluctant Grayson.

Goodman smiled and tried to pull open the door, but it was locked. Grayson gave a sigh of relief.

"Well, it looks like we won't be getting in through the front doors."

He started to walk back down the steps when a strong wind began to blow. The front doors swung open. Ethan held the door open.

"Well, that was interesting. Let's go."

They slowly walked through the doors and into the dark hallway of the school. Grayson was feeling a bit braver since they had made it inside, but he was still keeping his eyes open for any sign of the frogman.

As they crept down the hall, Grayson could hear a nervous Ethan ask, "Which door is the principal's office?"

Grayson had just realized that this was only the second day for Ethan. He had not gotten used to all the bizarre occurrences that happened at Hellman. JP came to an abrupt halt, and Grayson crashed into Goodman.

"Sorry," he said.

They were at the principal's door. JP put his hand on the doorknob and turned it. The door opened.

"It wasn't locked," said JP.

They entered the room. It was dark. Grayson was trying to find the light switch. He found it and turned it on. Even with the lights on, the room still looked creepy. Hanging on the walls were pictures of older principals, and on the wall behind Principal Schmitt's desk was a life-size portrait of her.

JP walked up to her desk and started opening drawers.

"Do you see where she keeps the keys?" asked Goodman.

JP opened several more drawers. "I don't see them. Maybe she takes them home with her."

Grayson noticed an ugly armchair sitting against the left wall. Above the chair was a small box with the word KEYS in bold, capital letters. Grayson approached the armchair, which looked like the skin of a bear. If he stood on the chair, he could reach the key box.

"I think I found where she keeps the keys," he said anxiously.

He climbed up onto the chair and opened the box. There were keys for each room in the building. At the very bottom of the box was a key marked "Master." Grayson took the key off the hook.

"I got it!" yelled Grayson.

The arms of the chair sprang to life, keeping Grayson in the chair. The key flew out of his hand and hit the floor. Grayson screamed as the grizzly bear head that was the top of the chair growled at him. Grayson could see the bear's sharp teeth.

"Why have you come to this office?" snarled the bear.

Grayson could feel the bear's claws digging into his ribs. He could also feel Goodman, JP, and Ethan's hands trying to pull the arms off him. Grayson could feel the bear's breath. It was hot and sour as it hit his face. The mouth was getting closer and closer to Grayson. Finally, the others were able to pull Grayson loose. The chair continued to growl and claw at the air.

Grayson backed up to the door, saying, "Now, that was scary."

Grayson noticed the look of horror on his friends' faces as they looked at him.

"I know it was scary, but I'm just fine."

Ethan slowly pointed to the door.

Grayson turned to see the frogman standing at the door. He backed up and almost fell into the chair, but Ethan had grabbed his wrist. Grayson could see the key; it was under the frogman. He could feel himself becoming angry.

Grayson's face was burning. He was sick of being scared and tired of running. He had had it.

"Stay away from me, you stupid frog!" screamed Grayson.

The frogman looked shocked to see Grayson running at him. Grayson dived and slid right between the frogman's legs, grabbing the key on his way.

Before the frogman had time to turn around, Grayson had kicked him in the backside. The frogman lost his balance and toppled onto the chair. Grayson could see the arms holding him, but the frogman was putting up a good fight. It wouldn't be long before the frogman would be able to get free.

"Head to the sewer!" Grayson yelled.

They ran for it, down the dark hallway into the cafeteria. The frogman had gotten out of the chair and was hopping after them. Goodman had made it to the door first. JP was right behind her, and they held the door open for Ethan and Grayson. JP and Goodman suddenly looked shocked. Grayson turned to see what they had seen and saw Ethan hit the trash cans.

Ethan fell to the floor with a loud thud. Grayson could see the spiders crawling toward Ethan. Ethan looked terrified as three huge spiders were trying to spin a web around him. He was frozen in fear as the frogman's long, pink tongue wrapped itself around Ethan's chest. Ethan flew toward the door. The frogman sat him down gently at Goodman's feet.

The frogman turned to Grayson and smiled. Then he hopped back into the dark hallway. Grayson was taken aback; he had expected the frogman to go after him. Once they all finally reached the door, Goodman shut it. They started walking toward the sewer.

Once they reached the sewer, Grayson bent down and unlocked the lock.

"Okay I'm going first, because I am ready to kick butt."

Ethan helped Grayson move the grate. Grayson jumped down, followed by Ethan, Goodman, and JP.

XVI

GOODMAN HEARD HER FEET SPLASH as she hit the floor of the sewer. She could imagine hearing what Amy would say if she knew Goodman was in the sewer. JP dropped in after her.

"Okay, now what do we do?" Goodman asked.

Grayson had walked a little forward. "It's a dead end," Grayson said.

The others joined him at the end of the short tunnel. This was puzzling to Goodman. She had seen Salmoa and Coach Sara go down this sewer.

"There has got to be a secret passage somewhere," she said.

Goodman started feeling the wall for a hidden door. Ethan was looking at the ground. JP was pulling at a stick that was buried in the mud.

Ethan gasped, "JP, no! It's a trapdoor!"

But Ethan was too late; JP had pulled the stick out of the mud. Goodman could feel the earth leave her feet, and she began to fall. She was sliding down a long, muddy slide. Her friends were yelling as they slid down as well. She was not sure, but she thought that she just might be the one in front.

It felt like she was falling for miles, but Goodman finally came to a stop. She was covered in muck. Standing up, she heard Grayson come to the end of the slide.

"Great, my mom is going to kill me for getting my clothes all muddy. She is always complaining about doing the laundry!" Grayson yelled as JP slid headfirst into his back.

Grayson and JP both got up as Ethan came to a stop. Ethan was not as muddy as the others. He stood up and wiped the mud off his pants.

"I was not sure I was on the same slide as you guys. I wasn't standing on the trapdoor. I saw you guys go down, then I decided to go down myself."

"Great," said JP. He was brushing the mud off his face. "Thanks for the warning. Has anyone thought of how we are going to get back up this thing?"

Goodman had been wondering the same thing. How were they going to get back to the surface? It had to be at least two miles up. There was no way they could make it back up the slide. She looked around the room. It was a large room with many tunnels going off in different directions. The room was lit by torches.

"Salmoa must be down that tunnel," said Ethan.

Goodman wondered how he knew this. He seemed to know the question going through her mind because he answered.

"It's the only tunnel that does not have torches around it, and Salmoa doesn't like heat."

Goodman looked around. It seemed that Ethan was right. There was only one tunnel without torches surrounding it. A thought came to her, and she voiced it aloud, "If Salmoa is down that tunnel, then what kind of creatures are down the rest of the tunnels?"

"Let's only deal with one monster today," said JP.

But Goodman had noticed a look of longing in his eyes. She knew that he was thinking that his brother could be down one of those tunnels. They began walking down the unlit tunnel. Grayson had the brains enough to pull a torch off the wall and bring it with him.

"Be careful with that torch. We don't want the fireworks to go off too soon," said JP.

Goodman was walking with Ethan. They came to a y in the path.

"Which way?" asked Ethan.

Goodman was not sure the tunnel was getting colder. She started walking down the left path. Grayson and JP had slowed down, so Goodman could not see very well.

"Are we sure about this?" asked Ethan.

Goodman was getting ready to answer when, for the second time, the ground vanished from beneath her feet. She felt Ethan grab her arm. The pathway had narrowed, and Goodman had not seen that the path had curved. She was dangling over the ledge.

Goodman could hear Ethan scream, "Help, she's slipping!"

Goodman felt her muddy arm slipping through Ethan's hands.

"Whatever you do, don't look down!" she heard Ethan call. She could now feel JP and Grayson grabbing onto her.

They were trying to pull her up, but they were all so muddy that they kept losing their grips. Goodman looked down and saw that she was high above what looked like a large ocean. But it couldn't have been filled with water.

It looks too thick to be water, Goodman thought. *It looks like blue slime.*

She felt JP's arms go under her armpits, and she was lifted up to the ledge. The others helped her to stand up, but none of them spoke. They were all staring out at the blue goo. Goodman thought that the slimy blue stuff smelled funny. It looked as if it had no end to it. Goodman could see that some of the other tunnels from the main room must have led to this room as there were other doors all around it.

"What is this place?" Goodman asked.

But it was not one of her friends that answered.

"This is the nexus of the bizarre," said an old, raspy voice. "It has been here for centuries. All of Hellman's strangeness comes from this place. Any of the bizarre events that have happened in the past or that will happen in the future all come from this place."

Goodman turned to see who was talking. A person, she could not tell if it was a man or a woman, was standing in the tunnel exit that they had just come from.

The person was dressed in a long black robe that fell to the ground. A hood made the face unable to be seen.

Goodman found her voice. "Who are you?" she asked.

Once again, the raspy voice replied, "Who I am is not important. What is important is that you leave this place before you join the rotting bones that litter the floor of these tunnels. I will give you one hour to get out and to never mention this place to anyone. If you have not left by then, the monsters that live here will destroy you. And trust me, there are worse things than Salmoa that live in this place." The person quickly left through the tunnel that they had come through.

"Who do you think that was?" asked Grayson.

Ethan looked at the floor, trying to remember something. "I have heard that voice before, but I cannot remember where I heard it," Ethan said.

JP was looking a little nervous. "I wonder what is down here that is worse than Salmoa?" he asked.

Goodman was in no mood to start going after whatever else might be down in the tunnels.

"Let's just get rid of Salmoa and get out of here," she said as she looked out into the glow of the blue slime. Goodman would be so happy to just leave it all behind, but she knew that the only way to get out for good was to get rid of Salmoa.

Walking across the narrow path together, Grayson was in the lead with the torch. They turned a few more corners and came to a large seaweed-filled room. Goodman could not see any sign of Salmoa. She could see a flight of stairs.

"Salmoa must be up there," she said.

There came a loud laugh, and Salmoa walked to the bottom of the stairs. "Welcome to my home. I hope you enjoy it because you won't be leaving—well, at least not alive." He threw his seaweed-covered arms into the air.

Ethan tried to run back, but the seaweed that had covered the floor was too fast. Goodman watched in horror as the seaweed slithered up Ethan's body. Grayson was holding the seaweed back with the torch, but there was water dripping from the ceiling, and slowly, the torch went out. Goodman was plunged into darkness.

Goodman could hear Grayson still fighting, but he became quiet as the seaweed took over him. Goodman was trying to find JP when she felt a slimy piece of seaweed grab her leg. There was nothing she could do but yell helplessly as the seaweed covered her mouth.

This is the end, thought Goodman as she couldn't breathe.

They had not even had a chance to attack. Now they would spend the last night of their lives in a muddy, old sewer underneath the school, and nobody would ever know what had happened to them. She closed her eyes as she felt the seaweed dragging them to their doom.

XVII

JP was sitting alone on the slide he had come down in the large room. He was covered in mud, slime, and blood. He was the only one who had gotten out of Salmoa's room filled with seaweed. JP was not quite sure how he had gotten out of the room.

JP remembered the seaweed wrapping around his legs. He also remembered hitting his head on stone. That wound was still bleeding. Somehow he had also been cut across the chest.

Sitting there with no way out, JP began to cry. He had failed. His friends were now doomed. Everyone who had either cared about him or he had cared about were gone. His parents would have lost a second son to the strangeness of the school. JP felt that he had let his brother down by never being able to discover what had happened to him.

JP felt useless. Why had he suggested that they come down here? A part of him was hoping that down in the sewers, he would find out the truth about his brother's disappearance.

Lying back into the mud, JP tried to listen for the screams of his friends, but all he heard was silence. Death was coming for him. If Salmoa didn't get him, then something else would.

"I deserve to die," JP said out loud. The tears were flowing down his cheeks.

"Now why do you think you should die?" asked a boy at one of the entrances to a tunnel.

JP sat up and looked at the boy. The boy looked a little older than JP, but he also looked just like JP, except for the fact that he had longer hair and wore glasses.

JP suddenly recognized his brother! He was not sure whether or not he was hallucinating. Maybe he had hit his head a bit harder than he thought.

"Oh, come on, little bro, you're the king of all the bizarre events that happen at Hellman. You know I'm real. This is not all in your head, although that does look like a pretty bad bump on your head," said Thomas, JP's older brother.

"What happened to you, Thomas? Why did you leave that night and never came back?" asked JP.

"I can't tell you all that, but I have no doubt that you will find out the truth in time. I am here to help you. Salmoa is a fierce monster. I will give you that," said Thomas.

"Is it Salmoa that got you?" asked JP.

"No, I was not one of his victims. There are many creatures that inhabit this place. But this is not even the place I died. Now then, let's get down to business. Your friends still have a chance if you have the guts," Thomas said emphatically.

"Of course, I have the guts!" exclaimed JP as he stood up. "I will do whatever it takes to save them. Just tell me how."

Thomas smiled, "You already know how to do it. You just need to get close to him."

"And how am I supposed to do that?" asked JP. "He has got all that seaweed."

"Sally almost got him. Come to think of it, she even had fireworks. She made it as far as the room with the nexus in it before he got her. Maybe she left her weapon there for someone else to find. Maybe it was meant for you to find it," said Thomas.

"What kind of weapon am I looking for?" asked JP

Thomas scratched his head, "I am not really sure, but you are a smart kid, you can figure it out. You have got to hurry as your hour is growing shorter, and you don't want some of these guys down here to get you. If you go up that passage, it will lead you to a secret way out." Thomas pointed to the path where he was standing. "Oh, and, JP, I am very proud of you, but you need to live your life. Don't worry about me. When it's time for the truth to come out, you will know. I love you, brother."

"I love you too," JP said as Thomas vanished.

He had gotten a sudden surge of energy. He had been allowed to talk to his brother and had been given a second chance to tell him good-bye.

"I will not let you have my friends, Salmoa. I am coming to get you," declared JP.

JP started to walk toward the nexus room. He knew he had to find the weapon that Sally was going to use. Grabbing three torches, he made his way to the room.

At the entrance to the nexus room, JP started looking on the ground for the weapon.

It must be something small, he thought.

He dug around on the ground for a little while and found it. He knew what he had to do. Picking up the three torches, he headed for Salmoa's lair.

As he came into the room with all the seaweed, JP tossed one of the torches onto a large pile of seaweed. The seaweed shriveled and was destroyed in a matter of minutes.

Laughing, JP went up the stairs, praying that his friends were still alive. He was going to save them. His plan was perfect. Soon it would all be over, and Salmoa would never hurt anyone again.

XVIII

ETHAN'S ENTIRE BODY HURT. OPENING his eyes, he saw that Salmoa was looking at him.

"Why, hello, little boy," said Salmoa. "How are you feeling? I will say I was right when I chose you to be my next source of food. You are quite tasty."

Ethan looked down and saw that he was in a seaweed-type cocoon. It went all the way up to his neck. Looking over, he saw Goodman and Grayson tied up with seaweed. It looked as if Grayson had been knocked out, but he was still breathing. Goodman had her eyes shut and was trying to take deep breaths through her gag of seaweed.

Salmoa got right into Ethan's face and said, "Does it hurt yet? I hope so. It really hurts to be electrocuted."

Ethan could smell his seaweed breath as he said, "You were trying to suck me into the closet!"

Salmoa gave a large smile. "Yes, if you had just come with me that night, I would have made it painless. I told you that I would take care of you. You are the one who had to make it painful."

Ethan tried to break out of the seaweed cocoon, but he was unsuccessful. "What is this thing?" he demanded.

Salmoa laughed. "That, my friend, is my life drainer. It's how I feed. You see, while you are inside of it, you are slowly dying. Your life flows into me. It takes about a year for someone to be fully drained of life. I have to feed on the lives of two children every five years. But this year, I'm getting lucky. I will get to feast on four children!"

Ethan looked around for JP but did not see him. "I don't see JP in here. Maybe you should learn how to count."

Salmoa lost his smile. "Don't worry about him. He will be next on the eating list." Salmoa clutched his left leg.

Ethan noticed a large bite mark on his leg. "What happened? Did JP bite you?" Ethan asked.

"No, this wonderful scar was made by your little friend over there," Salmoa said, pointing to Grayson.

For the first time, Ethan noticed that Grayson was not wearing a shirt. Salmoa seemed to be enjoying toying with Ethan.

"He was the reason JP got away. He was flinging that stupid torch around. I thought it had been extinguished, but at the last second, Grayson stomped, and some of the lit ambers floated into the air. He broke free, but instead of running away like JP, he attacked me, as if he had a chance. But I did get to see those wonderful fireworks," said Salmoa.

Salmoa pointed to the two bags of fireworks.

"He struggled when I tried to take them off. I had to knock him out. But he put up a really good fight. I still have some bruises, but you are healing them."

Salmoa went and sat down on what Ethan thought must be Salmoa's throne. It was a chair in the middle of the room that was covered in seaweed. Ethan also noticed that the lights in the room were from balls of the weird blue slime from the nexus. They were hanging from the walls.

Salmoa was looking at Grayson as he said, "You know, since you took a bite out of me, I may just take a bite out of you." Goodman was struggling with her bonds. "Don't bother, girl," said Salmoa. "It won't help you. If you two had not gotten in my way of getting the ones I wanted, then you would not have to be here."

Ethan let out a scream. He could feel the seaweed ripping at his bare chest and legs. It was so painful! Ethan just wished he could die. Salmoa was enjoying his pain.

He looked at Ethan and said, "Don't worry, the pain will only get worse. It will take a full year for you to die. But I have been thinking that I may not totally kill you. Since I have four children this year, I may drain you but, right before you die, let you go. Of course, I am sure one of my friends down here will enjoy snacking on your bones."

Ethan could feel the seaweed squeezing him inside the cocoon. He felt like his ribs were breaking, and it was getting harder for him to breathe.

"I still only count three," he said weakly. "JP is smart. He will find a way out of here."

Salmoa was laughing so hard that some of his seaweed fell off. "That boy, smart? You are dumb, aren't you? You were given one hour to get out of here. It has already been forty-five minutes. Even if you did escape, you would not make it out alive."

It happened suddenly. Salmoa doubled over and gave a loud scream. When he stood up again, Ethan could see black spots all down his side. Ethan also felt the seaweed around him loosen.

Salmoa walked over to Ethan. "Your little friend JP has just burned a pile of my seaweed. I'm sure he thinks that he is saving your life. I assure you, he is not. For every part of me that he burns, I will use you to heal!"

It happened again. Ethan could feel the seaweed on his bare back, legs, and arms. It was pain like no other; he hurt from his toes to the top of his head. He could feel the life being sucked out of him.

Salmoa yelled in pain a second time. More burn marks were covering his body. Ethan was ready for the pain to come again. He shut his eyes as the seaweed tightened. This time it only hurt for a moment. Salmoa had fallen to the ground for a third time.

Ethan once again could feel the seaweed loosen from his body, but he also felt his strength returning to him. JP had come into the room, holding one slightly burning torch.

"How's it hanging, Salmoa, old buddy?" he asked.

"You were foolish to come back here. You may have hurt me, but you will not be able to defeat me!" screamed Salmoa.

JP laughed. He threw the last torch at the seaweed throne. It burned to ashes. Salmoa screamed, but it soon became a laugh.

"That was your last bit of fire. Now you are at my mercy. I will enjoy draining the life out of you. However, I don't think I will use the life drainer. I will do it with my own teeth!"

JP looked worried. Ethan thought that JP's plan had gone wrong. Salmoa lifted JP off the ground by his neck. JP was kicking and trying to yell as the seaweed tightened around his legs. It was at his waist when Ethan saw that JP was not yelling, but he was trying to hide the fact that he was laughing!

There was a look of horror on Salmoa's face. He screamed, and JP fell to the ground. Ethan felt his strength return in full. He could feel the cocoon slowly falling off his body. His shorts had holes in them from where the seaweed had burned through. Ethan went over to Goodman as fast as he could. The seaweed had eaten through his socks and shoes.

Ethan broke through the seaweeds ropes and helped Goodman up. Grayson was starting to come around as they untied him. Salmoa was backing away in pain. JP was holding a silver cigarette lighter. He was using the small flame to back Salmoa into a corner.

Ethan was ready. He grabbed the two bags of fireworks and went to the center of the room.

"It's about to get really hot in here," he said, smiling at Salmoa. "And remember, you are the one who had to make this painful." Ethan took his and Grayson's shirts and put them over the two bags.

"It will only take about thirty seconds to blow," said Grayson.

Ethan looked at JP, "Will that give us enough time to get out?" JP nodded. "We win, you lose."

JP walked over to Ethan. "Would you like to do the honors, good buddy?" JP asked Ethan.

Ethan gladly took the lighter. "This is going to be fun!"

Salmoa's eyes were wide with fear. He tried to take a step backward, but he was too weak. He fell to the floor, saying, "Even if you kill me, you will never make it back to the surface. You only have one more minute until your hour is up."

Ethan lit the two shirts on fire then threw the lighter at Salmoa. The flame hit him in the chest. Goodman was helping Grayson as they started running to the exit. They made it into the nexus room when they heard the fireworks go off. They could hear Salmoa's screams all the way back to the big room.

Ethan could hear JP saying that he knew a way out. They came to a halt.

JP was talking, "It's right up those stairs." JP pointed to a tunnel.

The problem was that there was someone in the path—no, not someone, some thing.

It was huge! The creature had the body of a human, but it was all muscular. The head had only one eye and a huge nose. It roared at them. They could now smell the scent of burnt seaweed. The creature in front of them spoke, "You killed Salmoa!"

Ethan realized that this was not a question but a statement. The sound of other creatures approaching through the other tunnels could now be heard.

The creature spoke again, "I will now kill you!" It pulled an ax from behind its back. It began walking toward them but was stopped by a bright light.

The ghostly figure of Sally appeared, "Thank you for setting our spirits free. Hurry, there are more monsters coming."

They didn't need to be told twice. They ran down the tunnel as fast as they could. It seemed to take at least an hour to get back to the surface. Sounds of other creatures chasing them were heard the entire time they were running.

The tunnel they had taken led to the graveyard. They walked back to Ethan's apartment and were shocked to see that most of the damage caused by Salmoa had been repaired.

"Who do you think fixed it all?" asked Ethan.

No one answered him. They all went inside and fell asleep in the living room.

The next day, they got up and walked to school together. Their first shock of the day was to see Coach Sara walking by them in the hall.

She gave them a fierce look and said, "Get to class, you slackers."

Before going to their classrooms, they all agreed to meet at the steps to walk home together.

Ethan felt he could take on anything as he sat down next to Austin. Before class started, students were talking about a major earthquake that had hit the school last night. Austin had even said that the spiders' garbage cans had been knocked over and that they were rebuilding their webs.

Ethan was ready for the bell to ring when the principal walked into the room. She walked up to Ethan and Grayson's desks.

"Well, it's good to see that the two of you made it to class today. I hope that I will not have to warn you again to stay out of my office and to stay away from the sewer because next time, you may not be so lucky. Oh, and just a word to the wise, I would be very good in Coach Sara's class. You don't want to make her angry."

The principal straightened up and walked out of the door as the bell rang.

There were a hundred questions flying through Ethan's mind. He had just realized where he had heard that old, raspy voice. The principal knew that they were in the nexus room because she was the robed figure that had told them to leave!

Ethan was thinking, *Did this mean that the principal was a good person or just another bizarre part of the school? Everyone talked about the evil frogman, but didn't he save them from the spiders? How did Coach Sara get out of the sewer? What was that huge creature that was waiting for them at the exit?*

Ethan thought that it all must be part of Hellman Elementary. He smiled at Grayson and said to himself, "As long as I have good friends, I can make it through anything."

He knew that the next three years would be a strange adventure, but he was ready!

ABOUT THE AUTHOR

Richard Born grew up in Tennessee. He lived in Memphis until he started high school, when his family moved to Chattanooga. His enthusiasm for writing began in the third grade, and this continued passion was the basis for his high school teachers being forced to place a page limit on his assigned essays. After high school graduation and a year at the University of Tennessee at Chattanooga, Mr. Born made the decision to leave Tennessee to attend Western Kentucky University in Bowling Green. He majored in English, with the area of concentration in Creative Writing, and minored in Film Studies. While living in Bowling Green, he also became a foster parent to a number of children. Being a foster parent has given Mr. Born inspiration and insight into writing specifically for children. He has stated that their unique viewpoints on life's daily events—some good, some challenging—are certainly enlightening. He has also said that the children he has been a foster parent to have enriched his life with awareness and purpose of being there for others. He is a firm believer in foster parenting and adoption. Mr. Born has now returned to Tennessee, where he lives with his two sons and a dog named Bandit.

CPSIA information can be obtained
at www.ICGtesting.com
Printed in the USA
LVHW092307100519
617510LV00001B/29/P

9 781640 271531